BY FLAME

THE WITCHES OF PORTLAND, BOOK TWO

T. THORN COYLE

PF

Copyright © 2018
T. Thorn Coyle
PF Publishing

Cover Art and Design © 2018
Lou Harper

Editing:
Dayle Dermatis

ISBN-13: 978-1-946476-06-7

1

TOBIAS

Tobias had been fighting his demons since childhood. Fighting the voices that told him he wasn't good enough, and would never fit in. That he was stupid. Lacked ambition. Cried like a girl. And then, as he grew older, fighting the opinions that he was wasting his life.

The demons sounded an awful lot like his father.

Tobias stared out the window, past the shaking needles of the towering pine, at the rain-slicked street and cars shushing by. The morning's soft rainfall had increased, smacking harder on the window of the office space he rented in a large, three-story Craftsman. He turned from the window.

The office was small, but suited his needs. Tobias had settled in here six months ago, and it was finally starting to feel like home. He looked around his cozy space, at his favorite chair, dark brown, stuffed just right, and comfortable. A client chair, a wingback in deep blue and chocolate stripes, faced it across a small coffee table. The desk where he wrote up his notes and worked with his herbs was a long slab, a heavy oak door that he'd rescued from a sidewalk and propped up on two old filing cabinets. There were plants and jars of herbs on shelves everywhere, and seedlings under a grow lamp.

Between the herbs and the incense he burned at the office altar, the room always smelled good. Rosemary and thyme, verbena and datura, and the sharp undercut of vervain and some of the other nightshades, the herbs that grew in darkness under the light of the moon.

Usually just the scent of herbs made him want to work, but not today. Today, he felt restless, fractious. Brittle. He'd barely gotten through his meditation practice this morning, and had finally given up, deciding to just head to work, hoping that the change of scene would help.

Always awkward, often angry, Tobias stuffed his emotions down, deep inside himself, and simply got on with his life as best he could. But the emotions didn't go away. They just remained in hiding. And they still had way more control of Tobias's life than he wanted, even after an aborted attempt at therapy and after working with his coven for years.

It was getting ridiculous, and he knew it. Anyone else would say his life was perfect now. Perfect coven. Perfect home, with perfect housemates. Perfectly good herbalism practice.

"Go back to therapy, Tobias," Selene, one of his favorite coven mates, would say. "You were barely scratching the surface when you quit with Dr. Greene."

Selene was probably right. But still, Tobias didn't go. He was frightened of what he might find if he poked the shadows too often, or too hard. He had worked with Dr. Greene two years ago, when anger at his father started choking off his ability to tune into the herbs. It had helped. His healing ability had returned, at least.

But now? The demons seemed to be dancing around him again, and he wasn't even sure why.

That's a lie, he thought.

He fingered a small sunwheel made of woven straw. A Brigid's cross. He'd been making them all week, in honor of the Goddess he was dedicated to. It was her time of year.

The little solar cross was a distraction, but no comfort. Tobias was angry again; it simmered on a low flame, deep inside his stomach. All because his father had called, all politeness and judgment. Battering him down. Subtly sneering at his life. At the fact that he had housemates, instead of a down payment on a Pearl District condo.

Reminding Tobias that in his father's mind, he was a failure, and always would be. Oh, his dad said he was okay with Tobias being gay. He was a good liberal, after all. But he'd beaten Tobias for any perceived slight or weakness.

His father insisted on using his belt on Tobias's bare skin. It was more humiliating that way. The beatings had started because of Tobias's crying, but continued even after the tears had stopped for good. Tobias still had a scar, slightly raised and pale, where his left butt cheek met his thigh. One day, after Tobias had failed a biology test, his father had reversed the belt, smacking him—just that once —with the buckle. His mother intervened that day. The only time she ever had.

Bitch. His father was a grade-A major asshole, but his mother was frankly not much better. They were both snobs. And neither of them liked him very much.

So yeah, his life was perfect to anyone looking at it from the outside. Raised rich, with every advantage, in a fancy

Eastmoreland Tudor. Reed College for his undergrad. Pre-med.

But Tobias? He doubted that perfection every day. Not only had he rejected the family wealth, he kept waiting for the moment when someone would stand up, point, and shout "Imposter!" at him, revealing him to be what he was: just a mid-twenties white guy who didn't know what the hell he was doing.

He hid it well, most of the time. He had to. People didn't want to come to an herbalist for healing if the healer was a damn mess, seething with anger and unexamined emotions.

He was brooding again, when he should be working. Turning toward his office space, he looked around, trying to decide where to even begin.

A long row of woven solar crosses lined the back of the desk, leaning up against the white wall. He set the cross in his hands down in the empty spot he'd taken it from.

He didn't doubt the power of the herbs. Never had. The plants had wisdom he would never gainsay. He just doubted *his* ability to heal, to use the herbs the way they whispered that they wanted and needed to be used.

Because he couldn't heal himself.

Couldn't heal the aching in his heart that said he'd always be alone. Couldn't heal the anger that burned so many layers down even he could forget it was there half the time. Couldn't heal the alternating disregard and active disdain he got from his parents, and the dismissal from his aunt, who had set up a trust to fund his medical school tuition, when he told her he wasn't going after all.

"I want to study herbal medicine," he told her. Aunt Lydia had scoffed and told him he was on his own. She hadn't spoken to him since. Fine with him.

Well, here he was, at twenty-seven, and his business had

just barely tipped over into the black. Like the plants in his greenhouse, it was starting to thrive. He'd even been able to open his own small practice, not attached to the naturopath's where he had worked for a couple of years when he'd finished with herbalism school. New clients kept arriving, rain or shine, to ring his bell.

These were all things that should have proven the voices were wrong. That he had a chance to grow, and to heal. That maybe, just maybe, now was the time.

Tobias sighed. This introspection would keep for another time. He really needed to get to work now.

Everyone said what a great healer he was. "You have a way with herbs," Brenda, his coven mentor, said. "It's a real gift Tobias. Don't squander it."

Well, he wasn't so sure about that. All he knew was he had to keep working.

At any rate, today was another day. He had clients to see, formulas to concoct, and emails to answer. But first, as always, Tobias started his work day with prayer.

He turned toward his altar and took a deep breath, preparing to center himself. "Every act begins with breath," Brenda had told him when he first joined Arrow and Crescent. Ever since that day, he'd tried to be more conscious about it. To make breathing itself a practice.

The altar was a small, salvaged table covered with a white cloth, with a cast-bronze Brigid's cross that came from Ireland, a bowl of water, a small dish of salt, and whatever plant he was working with in the moment arranged on top. This week, the plant was thyme.

Okay, let's get on with this. He took another breath, *snicked* a match to flame, and lit the fragrant beeswax candle. He found his center, the place of stillness deep inside of him, his guiding post, his north star. Tobias reach out with his mind and felt the elements around him: earth, fire, air, water. He dropped and opened his attention, to feel the ground beneath him, the sky above him.

Silently, he prayed to Brigid to help him in his work. To center him. To make the anger go away.

When he finished, he felt calmer; at least, enough to shove aside the emotions and get to work.

He sat at the desk and flipped open his laptop. He always checked email to see if there were last-minute notes from clients before he started in on mixing new formulas from the tinctures he'd already prepared. He got to work, surrounded by the scent of the herbs. He scrolled through, clicking past advertisements, dragging things into the trash, and then he saw the notice.

The subject line just read "Sara." Sara was one of his clients. But he didn't recognize the email the note was coming from. He clicked, and his breath caught in his throat. It felt as though his heart would stop.

Oh no, Sara, oh no.

He knew it was possible of course; Sara had been very ill. She'd been working with Western doctors for years.

Tobias had helped her manage some of the side effects of the medications she was taking, and he knew he'd helped to ease her pain. But he'd really hoped, unspoken, but infused in every tincture, that this time he could save her. He'd hoped he would come across the right combination that would strengthen Sara to fight the disease that had her in its clutches. It hadn't worked.

"Sara died peacefully in her sleep last night," the note read. "I know she loved you, and loved working with you, and would have wanted you to know. Please let us know if there were any outstanding bills; we will pay her debts for her. She gave us so much in her life; we'll do everything we can for her in her death. I'll keep you updated on services. Best wishes, Jane—Sara's sister."

Tobias closed his computer, put his head in his hands, and began to weep, softly at first, then great gusts of tears and sound, loud enough to drown out the rain.

It was the first time he had cried since he was twelve.

2

AIDEN

It was a busy day at the soup kitchen. Aiden finished chopping up the last round of onions and went to wash his hands at the small sink by the long, white coffin freezers that held turkeys and hams. He dried his hands on the green apron he always wore.

"What do you need?" He turned to talk to Stingray, the crew chief. Stingray was a short, stocky Black woman, with a dark brush of hair crowning a square face.

"Why don't you go check out the floor?" she said, "I think the kitchen's pretty well done. We have plenty of people to serve the soup and salad today and some extra volunteers chopping up fruit for later in the afternoon. So we could really use another experienced body out in the courtyard, checking in with folks."

"You got it," he said.

Aiden grabbed a rag, just in case he needed to wipe up any spilled tea or milk, or crumbs from day-old muffins that some of the guests would bring in to share around. It always amazed Aiden how generous people could be—folks you'd look at and would think had nothing were often the first to share.

He walked through the brick-walled dining room, through the rust-colored metal doors, and out to the courtyard. There was an overhanging shelter with benches underneath it and a small patio area just outside with containers of plants and flowers and some herbs. He breathed in the scent of the wet plants and the rain, looked out at the stream of water drenching the flowers, and the leaves, and the concrete. Aiden gave a small prayer of thanks to God that he was alive another day.

Aiden had come to De Porres Catholic Worker as a lost young man. He'd run away from home because his parents couldn't stand that he was gay and he couldn't bear their rejection anymore. Their attempts to change him into something else. Their insistence that if he just prayed hard enough, God would change him back.

As though there was any "back" to change to.

Oh, they hadn't kicked him out of the house, and they never would. He knew they loved him in their way, but they didn't really love who he was, and he couldn't stand that anymore. Besides all of that, school had sucked. He came home bruised half the time and was sick of that, too.

Small-town Oregon life wasn't easy on freaks and losers, and Aiden was a bit of both.

So he'd run from Bend to Portland and found this place, this haven. It truly had felt like an act of God that brought him here. Out of all the missions in the city, the first place he tried was a place run by radical anarchist Catholics under the banner of the great, late Dorothy Day. They welcomed him immediately. After a long night of conversation, they figured out he was seventeen going on eighteen and convinced him to call his parents.

He told his parents where he was and that he wanted to stay, and they'd given their permission.

"At least you're with Catholics," his mother said. If that was what it took for them to not drag him back to Bend, so be it.

So he'd enrolled in his final semester in a Portland high school and had been with The Catholic Worker ever since, sleeping in his tiny room in the communal household, with its single bed and narrow dresser. He worked in the kitchen five days a week, opening the wooden gates each morning, letting the guests in, and serving them hot tea to drink while they waited for lunch. Then he would return to the kitchen to chop mounds and mounds of potatoes and carrots and garlic and onions and whatever other great things came in to add to the soup. He loved De Porres House. It was peaceful, and just what his soul had needed.

Even though sometimes he wanted more. Those days, he would go out to bars, just to be around other men, occasionally getting enough cheap beer into himself to risk a kiss or a dance.

Sure, it was a little weird, he guessed, for a twenty-two-year-old gay man to be working in a soup kitchen, but it was no stranger than any other occupation, and it felt right, like maybe he had a calling and that calling had been answered. Other times, he wasn't sure.

He still woke in the night sometimes, terrified, afraid of being beaten by the bullies at school. There'd been too many of those. His parents hadn't known how to stop them —they just told him over and over to pray harder and maybe God would make him not be gay anymore. As if. It was kind of unbelievable that people still thought that way, but plenty of them did. Not here at the kitchen, though. Here, he felt accepted.

"Hey Barry," he greeted a long time guest, a Black man who always carried spices in his back pack to liven up the soup. The soup was always tasty, but they couldn't make it too spicy—too many guests had stomach troubles. Living on the streets caused ulcers, he supposed. "How are things going?"

"Hey Aiden." Barry went to the tea urn, then settled on one of the long benches placed around the overhang walls. Aiden followed. "You know, cops been hassling the camp lately. Hope we don't need to move on soon. It's a nice spot."

"I hope so, too, man." One Heart was a long-established camp, where folks did their best to take care of the space and each other. They had community agreements and a loose structure, and had been successful at providing a home for the houseless for at least five years.

Aiden saw Mary Jo then, a white woman with layered sweaters under a long brown coat, and a sleeping bag rolled neatly at her feet next to a small backpack. She huddled over a book at one of the long tables, straggly brown hair falling over her face. The hair didn't quite cover the bruises on her weathered skin.

Aiden swiped his rag at some muffin crumbs, then shook it over a trash can and plunked the rag into a bucket of warm water on a cart near the rust painted doors. Then he headed to the metal tea urn himself.

Taking two of the heavy plastic cups, he filled them with the fragrant chamomile and spearmint combination and sat down in an empty chair across the table from Mary Jo.

There were other guests at the opposite end of the long table, but not close enough to listen if if Aiden talked quietly.

"Hey, Mary Jo, I brought you some tea."

Her brown eyes flicked up from the paperback, then back down again. She didn't lift her head.

"I just wanted to see how you were doing, and if you needed anything." He slid one of the steaming cups across the laminate wood table.

A pale hand with blunt fingernails snaked out from beneath the layers of sweaters and shiny brown coat and pulled the tea toward Mary Jo. She still wasn't looking at him.

"Do you want to talk about it?" Usually Aiden wouldn't ask. Guests were very private about their lives most of the time. They had to give too much up to social workers, police, hospitals, and shelters. Everyone had an opinion, but not many people had answers.

She shook her head.

Aiden could hear guests behind them starting to line up for food. Must be almost serving time. He had to get back inside to the kitchen.

"All right then, I'll leave you alone. But if you ever need anything, you let me know, okay?"

She finally looked at him, and the sorrow on her lined face just about broke Aiden's heart. "Thanks," she finally said.

Aiden nodded, picked up his cup, and stood.

"Hey man." It was Francisco, a Latino man who had been eating at the kitchen for as long as Aiden had been working here. He was always neatly dressed in work clothes. Aiden knew he had a delivery job that didn't quite make enough to feed the family toward the end of the month.

"Yeah?"

"Looks like there's trouble at the gate."

Aiden turned, and sure enough, there were two cops peering into the courtyard. A white man and a Black man.

The white man, the larger of the two, stepped through into the courtyard.

Aiden quickly set down his cup of tea, wiped his hands on his apron, raised his sweatshirt hood, and strode forward through the rain. "Excuse me, may I help you?"

"No, we're just here looking for someone."

"Well, you're not allowed to come in and look for someone, sir. I'm afraid I'm going to have to ask you to leave." The white man looked past him, as though Aiden didn't even exist.

Aiden's stomach muscles tensed, and he fought to keep his voice steady. The rain dripped down his face. He planted his feet wide and squared his shoulders, taking a deep breath. He hoped someone else from the kitchen would come out and back him up, but he couldn't leave to ask for help or the cops would be all the way in and who knows who they'd be hauling out.

"You're not allowed to impede our investigation, sir," the white cop said.

"I am allowed to ask you to leave private property."

The Black cop snorted. "Private property? I thought you were a bunch of anarchists." His fingers made air quotes around the last word. Both cops chuckled.

"Yes, yes we are. But a generous patron about fifteen years ago decided that De Porres House needed our own space and they *aren't* anarchists, so have no trouble buying property. They deeded the land and building to the kitchen and the people of Portland."

"Is that right?" the Black cop said. "Look man, we're just trying to do our job. Can you help us out?"

"I actually can't. The kitchen is a safe place for people. We're not allowed to cooperate with the police in making this anything *but* a sanctuary. People have to know that there's one place they can come and relax and get some food and not get hassled."

"Look man..."

"Please," Aiden said, holding up his hands, "I know you're just doing your job. But I hope you can understand that I'm also just doing mine."

"We can shove our way on past you."

"You can," Aiden said, "and then I can raise a stink in front of City Hall."

The cops sighed and exchanged a look. The white cop shrugged.

"Well, you take care," the Black cop said, and nodded at Aiden.

Aiden stood and watched them walk away. Once they cleared the gate, he exhaled, and all the tension left his body. He should have felt good, exhilarated, instead he felt exhausted.

He'd never thought he was good at standing up to people, but maybe, after all these years, he was learning.

"That's a good thing," he murmured to himself, "that's a good thing, Aiden."

Then he headed back inside. Lunch had started.

3

TOBIAS

Tobias felt defeated, like he'd been punched in the gut. His throat felt raw from holding back the tears. Thank the Goddess Brenda could meet with him. She said she would take a break from the shop and meet him at Raquel's café for lunch. The café was more public than Tobias would like, but he'd take what he could get.

He walked down the street, jacket hood up, head bowed to protect his face from the rain. The rain was relentless today. He usually loved it, but today, gray skies and falling water didn't feel like a thing he could enjoy. He couldn't enjoy the fragrance of the wet flowers he passed; he couldn't enjoy the sense of moisture in the air and the sound of the water washing away the oil and the dirt. All he could feel was that his own heart was breaking.

Sara's death had even eclipsed his father's phone call.

People have it a lot worse than you, you know. That's what he always told himself. But today? He didn't really care. The emotions he kept so carefully under lock and key had broken toward the surface, dragging loss with them, and the deep-seated sense of fucking failure. And anger at the way things were. And at the way his father still affected him.

Raquel's café was a warm, cheerful beacon as always. He knew she magicked it up, making it feel like a haven for people, a place folks could go to get some nourishment and rest. Raquel's heart was as big as her open arms.

He dragged open the glass-fronted door, nodding at a couple of people that he knew from the neighborhood sitting at one of the booths tucked against the wall under some bright paintings—abstract cityscapes this month. A riot of color and shapes.

As soon as he entered and slicked his hoodie off his head, Tobias felt a little better. Yep, that was Raquel's magic for sure. Something inside him relaxed slightly, so he could set down at least some of his burden. The café was warm. The smell of paninis grilling married with the scent of roasted coffee. There was a murmur of conversation, laughter.

"Tobias." Brenda's voice came from behind him. She was tucked up in a little two-top table, near the coffee condiments. Good, at least they wouldn't be sitting right next to other tables. They'd have some semblance of privacy. Looked like Brenda was already halfway through a panini. He gave her a small wave and approached the counter.

Cassiel, another coven member, was working the register, flaming red hair piled on top of her head as usual. She smiled at him, then frowned, "Hey Tobias, are you okay?"

He shook his head, "Not really, but I don't want to talk about it right now."

"That why Brenda's here?"

"Yes," he said.

"Good. What can I get you?"

He ordered his lunch and a cappuccino, paid, and made

his way to the table, squeezing past couples eating lunch and what looked like four local union members having a meeting over coffee. Everyone seemed as if they were in a good mood except him. He pulled back a red vinyl chair and sat, shucking off his coat and draping it over the back of his chair.

Sliding a napkin across his head and then his face, he wiped off the moisture.

"Thanks for coming," he finally said.

Brenda nodded, chewed, swallowed a bite of what smelled like a delicious ham, cheese, and spinach on grilled bread. "You want to tell me what's up?"

Brenda looked like a real witch. Or a psychic. Or like she ran a New Age store. Of course, all three were true. Her brown hair was piled up like Cassie's, but in a messy tangle, with tendrils cascading down to the silver moon-and-star earrings that set off the large moonstone pendant dangling at her neck. Bracelets and rings? She had them. Flowing purple and white layers of clothing? She had those, too.

"Cappuccino for Tobias," Cassiel called out.

"Gimme a second." He got his coffee in Raquel's signature red cup, and stirred a teaspoon of brown sugar in. It wasn't his usual drink, but he needed the comfort of the sweetness and the milk today. The sudden tears on top of his anger had shocked him almost as much as the news.

He sat back down and took a long drink and sighed.

"I feel like I'm... I dunno," he said. "I..."

Brenda just looked at him and took a sip of her own coffee, "Just tell me, Tobias. How long have I known you?"

"Years," he said.

"Years," she agreed.

"My client Sara died. I just found out today."

"Oh sweetie, I'm so sorry." She reached a hand out and

squeezed his. He gave her a squeeze back and then, wisely, Brenda went back to her sandwich.

Brenda knew to give him time. She was mentor to a lot of people in the coven. She would always have a special place in his heart for the way she kicked his ass when he was acting out during his first year with the Arrow and Crescent Coven. He needed it, just like right now he needed a shoulder and maybe another ass-kicking.

"Tobias, what do you need from me?" Her voice was gentle, but she was clearly tired of his silence.

"I need you to tell me I'm not a failure."

She gave a huff of impatience at that.

"How many times are we going to have to have this conversation?" she said. The kindness in her eyes took a little bit of the sting from her words. "Tobias, you are a healer and sometimes people still die. It doesn't mean you're not gifted, it just means that's how life works. You know that."

"I know, but I..."

"No, you don't know," Brenda said, putting a little heat behind her words. He felt the push of them against him, as if she'd used some of her formidable power.

Cassie set his sandwich down in front of him, squeezed his shoulder, and went back behind the counter. He really didn't feel like eating now.

Brenda continued, "Life and death and life again. You learned that your *first year* with the coven. Everything cycles, everything changes, and not everybody can be saved in this incarnation. Besides, you don't know what this person's work was. You don't know whether or not they fulfilled it, and you don't know what the next part of their journey is."

"I know you're right, but it doesn't feel that way." He felt his face flush with anger. "It feels like if the Gods really gave me these gifts, I should be able to *do* something with them, something more than what I'm doing. Something more than just helping a bunch of middle-class white people maintain their horrible lifestyles and work themselves half to death. Or the ones that are actually trying to heal, but, well, they just end up dying anyway."

He knew he sounded like a petulant child and he didn't really care. He was pissed off again.

Brenda took another bite of her sandwich and chewed. Her eyes never leaving his own. He finally looked away and picked up his own sandwich, even though his stomach was cramping up. He just needed something to do. He needed to avoid Brenda's all-seeing eyes. *You called this upon yourself*, he thought, chewing the sandwich. He could barely even taste it.

"Tobias, you take everything too hard, and you take everything too hard because you want to think you're in control. And anytime you think you're out of control, you get angry and frustrated and you beat yourself up about it. You *do not run this world*," she said, leaning across the table. "You need to learn to let things go."

"But how?"

"Are you centered right now?" Brenda asked.

Tobias paused, closed his eyes, and checked in. "No, I don't even know where my center is."

"Well, that's just laziness. You do know where it is. You're choosing not to connect. I suggest you take a day and get your house back in order."

He opened his eyes. "What do you mean?"

"Well, you called me for a reason. The coven needs you. Your clients need you, and looking at you now, I've got a feeling there's an even greater need that's going to come knocking on your door any minute now. I can feel it around your head. You need to be prepared for that or you're going to stumble and fall, and that really *will* be a failure."

Brenda took a sip of coffee, eyes never leaving his face. He started to say something, anything, but she held up one hand to stop him.

"You can choose right now to go back to the basics, center yourself, figure out your boundaries, and remember why you chose to work as a healer in the first place. It's not just that you're gifted. The gifts are the easy part. Always. It's what we choose to do with them that matters."

Oh shit, he thought. She'd just busted him and he wasn't even sure how.

"Okay, you're right," he finally said, just to say something. Even though his mind and emotions were still a roiling mass of confusion, a small part, deep inside him could feel that she was right.

"Eat your sandwich, healer," Brenda said.

He held her gaze for one more moment. Then picked up half of his panini and took a bite.

"And Tobias? That therapist of yours that Selene is always after you to go back to? Now might be a good time."

Yeah. Maybe.

4

AIDEN

The church was dim and cool, verging on cold. Aiden wrapped his sweater around himself a little more closely, and wound the wool scarf back around his throat. He'd flung his jacket beside him in the pew. It was damp with rain, the same rain streaming down the stained glass windows on either side of the sanctuary. Aiden wasn't concerned with that; the rain was a constant in Oregon.

What he was concerned with was the fact that he felt angry. Anger wasn't a feeling he enjoyed. At all.

He scooted forward on the pew and knelt down. The damp knees of his jeans hitting the padded kneeler, he gazed up at the cross above the white marble altar.

Jesus, the one he couldn't quite walk away from, even though the pain of rejection still stung. He knew that a lot of the church teachings were fucked up. He couldn't quite let the church go, though, so here he was, trying to find a space for himself in the place his childhood self still adored.

"I don't know how you can help me," he said. He spoke quietly, even though he was the only one in the sanctuary that late winter afternoon. The encounter with the cops had shaken him really badly. He'd never stood up to someone like that before. He'd seen other people do it, the more experienced soup kitchen workers; they were pretty badass.

"You're tenderhearted," Stingray would tell him, "and that's a good thing, don't lose that."

"But I need to be strong," he replied.

"You can be strong and tenderhearted at the same time. They're not mutually exclusive. Besides which, you think anyone of us would be here if we weren't tender-hearted?" Stingray laughed. He laughed along with her, but at the time he didn't really understand. After today, he wondered if that wasn't part of what she was talking about.

Help me, he thought. *Help me out.* He paused. *Help me out of what?* he asked himself. He hadn't thought of that construction before, that when you asked someone to "help you out," that maybe you were asking them to take you away from something, or to help you slide out of the hole you were stuck inside.

He felt stuck inside of this emotion. This anger. Aiden wasn't just slightly pissed off. He felt enraged, actually. As though he could flay something alive with the anger. Kill something, even. After the cops had left, he'd told Stingray and a few other key volunteers what had happened. Then he'd joined the dish line, which had been short-staffed.

All through his shift, all through cleanup, the anger never left him. He wasn't sure what he was even angry at. It was the cops, sure, but his anger felt like overkill.

It was something deeper. Something he couldn't quite name yet. And he didn't like the feeling. Not at all.

The bruised and battered figure on the cross looked down at him. A victim of state torture and state execution, if anyone would understand the predicament Aiden was in, surely Jesus would. He had plenty of encounters with the cops of Rome.

But the figure remained silent. Aiden's heart heard no voice. And even though the church itself felt *comfortable* enough—familiar, even safe—today it wasn't comforting at all.

His fingers gripped the wooden edge of the pew, digging into the hard oak. Today he wanted to punch something, he wanted to rail and rage, but there was no outlet for that. Aiden was a good boy, even if he was a faggot. He was still that Catholic kid who wanted to do right. Standing up to authority like that? That was a no-no.

"*You* stood up to authority, though," he said to the mute statue hanging on the wall. "What did you do with your anger? Did you ever feel this way?"

The statue seemed larger than life, even though Aiden knew it wasn't even life-sized. It loomed over the white marble altar, pierced feet pointing toward the tabernacle with its closed brass doors.

A priest came out onto the altar, genuflected, and started fussing with something at the lectern. Getting ready for vespers, maybe? Did this parish even have evening services? Aiden didn't know. But the presence of the priest wasn't going to help his prayers any.

"Ah, screw it," he muttered, and grabbed his jacket. Genuflecting quickly towards the altar, he walked his way to the back of the church, ready to go out again into the pouring rain.

Then a glint of colored light caught his eye and he turned his head to the left. And there she was, blue sky behind her head, a flame cupped in the open palm of her left hand, a woven cross of wheat straw held in the right. He stopped dead in his tracks, struck by the image.

"Who are you?" he asked. But he knew. Of course he knew. St. Brigid. Mary of the Gaels. There was a legend that she had been taken by angels to the Holy Land, and acted as midwife to Mary herself. She took care of people. She stood up to landowners. She was said to have healing powers.

And she apparently liked beer, if he recalled correctly.

Aiden didn't know how much of that was true. The whole going-to-Bethlehem thing couldn't be. All he knew was there was something here, in the image of this woman, something he hadn't felt up at the altar. He felt it staring at this figure, at the woven cross in her hand and the flame cupped in her palm.

Maybe she would understand.

"Brigid, healer, caretaker. You of the green mantle, you of the holy flame and the sacred well, help me. Help me please. I have such anger inside of me today, I don't know what to do with it all."

He didn't even know where the words were coming from. He'd never prayed to this saint before in his life. He wasn't much of a saint-prayer in the first place; that was his mother. But here, in this church on this rainy February afternoon, it felt like all he could do was pray.

He started to feel lightheaded, a little dizzy, staring at the image. It was as though the brown eyes of the saint were boring their way into his own head. He felt caught by the glass gaze. How was that possible?

A sharp pain pierced his heart, as if someone had touched a match to his skin. All of a sudden, his chest felt as if it were on fire. He dropped his jacket and clutched his heart. *I'm too young for a heart attack*, he thought. *What's happening? What's happening to me?* The flames grew stronger and stronger, engulfing his whole body.

He fell to his knees. He heard a clatter and a shout from the altar just as he collapsed to the ground.

"Brigid, Brigid, Holy Brigid," he panted out. His hands scrabbled at the old brown carpet and then he fell all the way down, remembering to turn his face before it struck the floor. He felt the rough nap of the carpet on his cheek. He was sobbing, on fire. His heart was being ripped out from beneath his rib cage by hot metal pincers.

A hand gripped at his shaking shoulder, and everything went black.

5

TOBIAS

Tobias had a client coming in thirty minutes and he needed to prepare. His work space was in order. He'd fluffed the deep teal throw pillow on the client chair and made sure the small coffee table was cleared.

The only thing that wasn't clear were his roiling emotions. It had been another crappy-meditation morning. He felt sour, like the taste of this morning's grapefruit juice. Raquel would tell him there was no such thing as good or bad meditation, that meditation just *was*, neutral. Yeah, but some days still felt better than others.

Just like some days he tuned in easily to the plants, and other days, he just couldn't get through. Today? He had to keep trying. His clients depended on him.

The call from his father still rankled. Combined with the news of Sara's death, and Brenda's sharp words, the memory of his father's voice threatened to throw him into a shame and anger spiral.

It was time to turn to the altar. Do some cleansing. Again.

He lit the candle and touched a stick of Nag Champa

incense to the flame. Once the end was glowing orange, he blew out the flame, allowing the earthy scent of sandalwood and plumeria to wreath around his head. He breathed it in, then placed the stick in a long wooden holder that would catch the ash as the stick burned down.

After three attempts to slow his breathing down, he finally was able to get a steady, even flow of air entering and exiting his lungs.

His emotions slowly calmed. His head began to clear.

When he felt ready, Tobias took another breath and spoke into the room.

"Holy Brigid, fiery arrow. You who work the forge that makes us true. You who tend the well of healing, and the fires of inspiration, inspire me now. Heal me now. Forge me now. Be with me, work through my hands so that I may heal. Work through my mind so that I may know. Work through my voice so that I may speak, and work through my heart so that I may listen to the things that the mind cannot yet know. Holy Brigid, be with me now."

He gave a little bow towards the altar. He knew the Goddess wasn't there, not on the altar itself, but Brenda and Raquel always said that going through the motions helped alert the parts of the soul that weren't rational.

"Those are the parts that art and music touch," Raquel would say. "Those are the parts that learn through dancing, or learn through the things that you already know how to do, like listening to plants. The rational mind can't comprehend it, but that doesn't mean it isn't real."

Tobias was *still* learning to trust that, despite having seen the truth over and over again. As a member of the Arrow and Crescent Coven, and as an herbalist, he'd experienced things directly that his mind still railed against, and his emotions sneered were childish or impossible. But he knew all of that wasn't him. It was the demons inside of him that wore his father's face.

"Brigid, give me strength. Help me to be of service to this world."

Good enough for today, at least, and just in time. There was a knocking at his door.

He opened it and looked up. Where he expected to see his client, Janice, instead his father and mother stood in the hallway. His father wore a tan trench coat. The tightly closed black umbrella in his right hand probably cost more than Tobias paid for groceries in a month.

His mother wore a bright green raincoat, whose sale could have likely paid his rent. Her dark hair was perfectly styled, as always, despite the spitting rain. She smelled of Chanel No. 5.

What in the nine worlds were they doing here?

Boundaries, Tobias. He sent a long, slow breath outward, imagining it tracing the edge of his aura, reinforcing his space.

"I'm sorry, I don't have time for you today," Tobias said. "I've got a client coming any second now."

"The timid woman? Blond hair and some sort of puffy jacket? I sent her away. Told her there was a family emergency."

"You *what?*"

His father shouldered him aside. Tobias's mother at least had the grace to look apologetic as she followed him.

"Wait here," Tobias said, then ran down the broad wooden staircase, and out onto the broad front porch. No Janice. Damn it.

He forced himself to not slam the heavy wood door. No need to piss off the other tenants of the space. His footsteps were heavy on the stairs.

Opening his office door, he saw that his mother had seated herself in the wingback chair, but his father was still standing, peering at his altar.

Anger flared inside Tobias. How dare he?

"What the hell do you think you're doing?" Tobias spat out. He was practically vibrating. All the emotions he'd just gotten under control ten minutes before had risen to the surface like a nest of writhing snakes. Or the sparks of a bonfire, flaring in the night.

His father tsked. "Don't talk that way to the man who pays your rent, son."

That stopped Tobias cold. His head whipped from his father to his mother. She glanced at him, then turned her gaze toward the big windows. Right. No help from that quarter, as usual.

"What are you talking about?"

His father didn't answer, just turned slowly, taking in the shelves of bottles, plants, and herbs, the old wooden case that held tinctures that were in process or were ready to be mixed into specific combinations for his clients, swept back, lingering a little too long on the small altar, and then to Tobias's face.

"I own that house you live in, you know. Why do you think your rent is so cheap?"

Fuck. No. No way.

Tobias dragged the wooden chair out from underneath the slab of his desk and sat.

"How long?"

"How long have I owned it? Oh, since around six months before you moved in."

"But Freddie..."

His father laughed. "Freddie's father is an old golf friend. Didn't he tell you? I offered Freddie the place for a song if he wouldn't tell you about it. Told him to contact you about a room for rent."

Tobias stared, unspeaking, at the row of Brigid's crosses on the back edge of his desk.

"What?" his father continued. "You didn't think I would let my son actually struggle too much, did you? But I think we've let this little experiment go on long enough, don't you?"

Tobias's skin flared with fire, then ice, then fire. He wanted to puke. "What are you talking about?" Those seemed to be the only words he had left.

"I think it's time you went back to school and studied something real. I thought you wanted medicine, but if you want to come into the family firm instead, I'm happy to teach you the ropes. You could get an MBA at night. Or just learn the business as you go."

"Trade stocks? Investments?"

His mother stood then, and placed a soft white hand on his arm. It took all he had to not shake her off.

"There are worse ways to make a living, Tobias. We just want what's best for you," she said.

Tobias stood suddenly, throwing his mother off balance. She stumbled into his father.

"Did you just shove your mother?"

"No, Jim. I was just startled..." she said.

"Did you?" The familiar tone was back. And the familiar flushing of his father's cheeks.

The scent of incense filled his nose, and the flame of the altar candle flared up, three inches high.

Tobias remembered who he was.

"I don't hurt people," he said. "That would be you. I've got the scars to prove it. Remember, Father?"

"Tobias..." His mother held up a hand.

"Enough, Mother. Don't you think? Don't you think it's *enough* now?"

She fell silent.

His father reached around her and grabbed Tobias's arm. "You ungrateful faggot."

"Thanks for telling me how you really feel, *Dad*." He pulled his father's fingers from his arm. "Now get out of my office. Both of you."

"You'd better start thinking about a new place to live, son. You're about to get quite the rent increase."

"Well, I'll be calling the Tenants Union then, won't I? We'll see how long I can get away without paying any rent at all."

His father shoved him against the desk. It slammed against the wall.

Then he yanked open the door and strode out.

"Clara? Come!"

"Call me if you need something," his mother whispered, and with a swish of her green coat, she was out the door.

Tobias carefully shut the door behind her.

Then he turned and, arm stiff as a knife, swept everything from his desktop. Brown bottles waiting to be filled. Client files. An aloe vera plant. It all went crashing to the wooden floor.

One more sweep of his arm, and with a shush and a scrape, the small straw sun-wheels fell, too.

Tobias's breath heaved. He was sweating.

Looking at the wreckage at his feet, he found that he didn't feel any better. But he also knew it had to be done. This destruction.

He'd avoided destruction for years. Kept the leash wound tight. Well, he was done with that now. Fuck his parents. Fuck playing it safe anymore.

The candle on the altar died back down again. It flickered and winked at him. The stick of Nag Champa had burned itself halfway down.

Tobias dropped into his favorite stuffed chair, sinking into the upholstery. Drawing his phone from his pocket, he pressed the button for his contacts, scrolled, and dialed.

After three rings, someone picked up.

"Hello. This is Tobias Kenner. I'd like to make an appointment with Dr. Greene. First available opening, please."

Maybe it was time to get back into therapy after all.

6

AIDEN

T he nightclub was jammed with men, the scents of sweat and cologne mingling with beer and whiskey. *Boom, boom, boom, boom*—the bass thrummed through Aiden's body.

He couldn't really afford to come out and drink beer tonight, but after his encounter with the cops, and then his weird experience in the church, Aiden needed something to take him out of himself. He could still feel the panicked priest crouched over him, patting at his cheeks with holy water. He shook himself, as if he could slough off the whole thing.

He needed a distraction; he needed the release of music and dancing, maybe a beer or two.

Anything to avoid thinking about what exactly had happened in the church. Anything to take away the burning feeling in his chest, and the memory of those brown glass eyes staring into him.

Blue LED lights chased each other at the back of the long bar, dancing in time to the music. The bar was three deep in men, despite it being a weeknight. A bartender, all pomaded hair and muscled arms, spun bottles in his hands, mixing cocktails, then twirled to snick the caps off bottles of beer. A second bartender was working the taps, filling pint glasses with amber liquid, occasionally pouring out a shot of whiskey or tequila.

And then Aiden saw him—a whip-thin man at the end of the bar—dark brown hair, couple shades darker than Aiden's own framing his face, falling softly past his jaw line. He had a little goatee and what looked like kind brown eyes. He was just Aiden's type, if Aiden could be said to have a type. Working in a soup kitchen, he didn't really date much. He didn't have money to go out very often and the only men he regularly met were houseless, or other workers at the kitchen, or businessmen who scoffed at his scruffiness and his lack of money. Aiden didn't need that.

"What can I get ya?" a voice startled him out of his reverie. It was the second bartender. He was a nice-looking man too, heavily muscled, tight tank top, his dark brown skin framing deep black eyes. His head was shaved.

"Um, whatever's on tap, just a beer."

"Great." The bartender tilted the pint glass under a tap, topping it off with a layer of light foam. He slid it across the bar.

"How much?" Aiden asked.

The bartender considered him carefully.

"How much?" Aiden asked again.

"You work at that homeless shelter, right?"

"Soup kitchen," Aiden said.

"I thought so. I've seen you around the neighborhood. Tell you what, this one's on the house. You can give me a bowl of soup someday."

"Thanks man. That's great."

"No prob." The bartender smacked his palm on the bar

and walked away to the other customers who were clamoring for drinks.

The music shifted again, and the blue lights reversed themselves. Michael Jackson started singing about starting something. Aiden smiled. Maybe coming here had been an okay idea after all. He sure would like to dance, forget himself for a while, forget the cops and the weirdness of a saint looking into his eyes, and that strange heart-attack feeling of being on fire.

The priest had asked him if his left arm had gone numb. It hadn't, and Aiden didn't know if that was good or bad. The priest let him go only when Aiden promised to stop by the clinic. Well, by the time Aiden got out of there, the free clinic was closed. He felt okay. He actually felt more than okay. He felt like something had changed, but other than his fury having crawled back to a reasonable mixture of sadness and anger at the way of the world, he didn't know what.

He sipped at his lager, letting the cool beer wash down his throat, and smelled the mingled scents of the men nearby—Polo Black, Old Spice, and sweat. He wondered what the man at the end of the bar smelled like. His feet seemed to move on their own as he angled his shoulders and squeezed through the crush of men, letting Michael Jackson carry him forward.

"Hey," he said.

"Hey." The man looked at him. Aiden felt a shock down to his toes. It was as if he'd stuck his finger into an electrical socket. What in the world was happening to him today?

"My name's Aiden," he finally croaked out and took a quick swallow of beer, trying not to choke. The man smiled. He had a beautiful smile.

"Tobias. I'd offer to buy you a beer," Tobias said, "but it looks like you're well set."

"Yeah, yeah, the bartender gave it to me."

"Wow, that's a miracle here. Bartenders here don't give anyone anything. He must like you."

Aiden just shrugged. He didn't know how to respond. He didn't have much practice with banter or flirtation, so he took a deep breath, trying to calm his nerves.

"So, what do you do, Tobias?" he asked. He couldn't believe he was asking someone what they did for work. What a dumb opener.

"I'm an herbalist," Tobias responded.

"Wow. That's actually interesting."

Tobias smiled. "Yeah, yeah, it's pretty cool most of the time."

Aiden noticed that the smile didn't quite reach Tobias' eyes.

"So, like, what does that mean?" Aiden said, "You help people, you grow plants? What do you do?"

"Both. At least I try to."

As they talked, Aiden's eyes kept flickering from the man's mouth to those deep brown eyes. He felt like he could trust this man, at least he hoped so. Finally they both finished their beers.

"Wanna dance?" Tobias asked.

"I'd love to."

They moved their way through the crowd to the thumping dance floor, Beyoncé now. Everybody loved Beyoncé. Aiden started to dance, a little awkward at first.

Tobias bumped up against him and smiled. Aiden cut him a quick smile back. The lights—blue, white, and amber —flashed over Tobias's face, sparking on his cheekbones, shadowing his eyes.

He smelled like church. Like frankincense and myrrh. Aiden reached out and touched the other man's arm, just above his elbow. Tobias reached up and laced their fingers together. Just the one hand. Half connected, half free.

As the two men moved together, Aiden felt something inside of him loosen and let go. He slid his hand from Tobias's and raised his arms above his head. Then he leaned a little closer. He could still smell Tobias—woven with the traces of incense, he smelled like breath mints and warm skin. A little bit of the hoppy scent of beer still lingered on his lips.

Aiden wanted to kiss those lips. He leaned away again. No, no, no Aiden, don't fall in too soon.

His chest grew warm. A tingling ran along his skin. The music hummed and pounded through his feet, his hands, his thighs, and his chest. The pulsing rose and snaked toward the back of his head. The music filled him, all the way up. He felt the man moving in front of him and the other men bumping him, shoulders, hips, and butts. He loved the crush of it; he loved feeling held this way—held by music and a moving throng of men.

A smile touched Aiden's lips and he felt as though he was about to cry.

Then his chest caught fire again, and he fell into Tobias's arms. His lips found the other man's waiting. Rough. Strong. Open.

Pure.

7

TOBIAS

Tobias was aware of the soft flannel sheets draped around his naked body, and the heavy layers of blankets beneath the comforter. Crows called to each other outside the window, and a squirrel chattered. No sound of rain, though that wouldn't last for long. It was *freezing* in his bedroom. The temperature must have really dropped in the night.

Tobias rolled onto his back and blinked up at the pale blue ceiling of his bedroom. His nose and ears were cold, but the rest of him was warm. He also felt exhausted. The emotional upheaval was taking its toll. If he didn't have a stack of work waiting for him, he'd be tempted to curl up in bed all day, drinking cups of tea and reading novels.

He hadn't let himself do that for a long time. There was always work to be done when you ran your own business. But maybe he needed a mental health day, like Brenda said. He began to go over his schedule in his head. Did he have any clients actually coming in? Or was he just filling orders?

Too sleepy to remember. He'd have to actually get some tea into himself and look at his calendar. The one thing he knew for sure was that the coven had ritual tonight. It was Imbolc. He didn't know if he could face the coven, or Brigid. Sure, he'd called Dr. Greene, but he was still pretty pissed off, including at the Goddess.

The light in the room was gray. Turning his head, he let his eyes wander over the three framed botanical prints hung on the deep green wall. Yellow yarrow. Pink foxglove. Blue aconite.

Then he became aware of something else, the soft sound of someone breathing next to him. He turned his head, and there he was, the man from the nightclub—Aiden. The man who had kissed him so intently on the thrumming dance floor. The man he had taken home and kissed some more.

There'd been a lot more than kissing last night. The room still smelled faintly of sex. It mingled with the wisps of frankincense and myrrh Tobias always burned on his bedroom altar.

The sound of water running in the bathroom down the hall meant that his housemates were up and getting ready for work. His housemates. Traitors. He hadn't confronted them yet. What was he even going to say to Freddie? And how was he going to pay whatever the increased rent turned out to be?

He would need to talk with Cassiel about Tenants Union stuff. She'd had a tussle with her landlord that had ended up with her losing her apartment, but not until the coven helped expose a bunch of dirty dealings between landlords, developers, and the city.

Arrow and Crescent to the rescue.

Tobias exhaled, and went back to looking at the treat curled up so sweetly in his bed. The man looked beautiful in his sleep, dark eyelashes framing his closed eyes. Those eyes that Tobias knew were a piercing blue.

That was one good byproduct of Tobias's outrage, at least. The heat of it needed to go somewhere, and if Tobias couldn't punch someone, and didn't want to wreak more havoc on his office, he'd known he at least needed to go out dancing and drinking to spend some of the frenetic energy.

The result had been pretty good this time. He'd actually brought home a man he wanted to see again.

Those blue eyes had stared directly into Tobias's as they had made love, as though they could ferret out his secrets. Tobias supposed he shouldn't call what they'd done making love. You pick up a man in a nightclub—where you've gone to fuck because you can't fight—and you take him home, that's about sex, not love.

But *making love* was the phrase that came to mind nonetheless. And wasn't that a surprise? Maybe Aiden was more than just a fuck.

He wanted to roll onto Aiden and start all over again. Beginning with the amazing kissing part.

Instead, he snaked a hand out from beneath the layers of blankets and comforter, and gently petted the shock of seal-brown hair falling over Aiden's face. He was so pale against the burgundy sheets—must be Irish blood.

Aiden inhaled sharply through his nose, then his eyes snapped open. "What, what?" Aiden looked around confusedly, then his eyes lit on Tobias's face and he blinked. "Oh. Right."

Tobias grinned. "Right. Good morning. Your name is Aiden, my name is Tobias. You came home with me last night."

"Huh." A red stain crept up Aiden's cheeks. "I, uh, yeah. I don't usually do this. Uh, no, as a matter of fact... um..." He coughed, then smiled a little ruefully. "This may have been a first."

Tobias leaned over and kissed Aiden's sweet lips, "Well, I hope it won't be the last."

"Oh yeah. Yeah, that too. I mean, I hope that too."

"Can I make you some coffee? Tea?"

"What time is it?"

Tobias fumbled around the nightstand for his phone, "Seven thirty-five."

"Shit." Aiden scratched his head, hard, as if he was trying to get blood flowing to his brain.

"What's the matter?"

"I have to get to the kitchen."

"You go to work this early?"

"Yes." Aiden was already out of the bed, fumbling on the floor for his boxer shorts and jeans.

"You need to borrow some long underwear or something? I think it's freezing out."

"You're telling me. No, I'm good. I'll run by my house on the way in."

"You sure I can't get you some coffee?" Tobias climbed out of bed himself, shucking on his own briefs and jeans, pulling a T-shirt on over his head. "Or you need a shower or something?"

"No, no, man, I'm good."

Aiden was clearly uncomfortable. He could barely look at Tobias. Tobias hoped this didn't mean the end; he really liked the man, which didn't happen often. He looked at his bedroom altar, at the statue of Brigid, the votive candle in front of it, unlit, the metal dish for incense, all of it waiting for him to say his morning prayers.

Did you have something to do with this? he thought. He wouldn't put it past her. Brigid didn't usually meddle in affairs of love, or sex for that matter, but love was healing wasn't it? Who knew with the Gods and Goddesses? It was hard to say *what* they were going to get involved with or not.

If you did, thank you. Even if I'm still pissed off.

When he turned, Aiden was sitting on the edge of the unmade bed, lacing up his boots.

"Can I see you again?" Tobias asked, leaning against the foot of the bed, rubbing the goose bumps from his arms. "Can I buy you dinner sometime?"

Aiden whipped his head around, his blue eyes still looked startled, a little haunted, a little hunted perhaps. Tobias saw the man look at his altar, a strange look on his face.

"Um, yeah, sure, that would be great."

"Okay." Tobias picked the rain jacket that Aiden flung on the back of the chair when they'd hurried out of their clothes.

He handed it out to Aiden, who zipped it up and wrapped a long navy scarf three times around his neck.

"Um, well, Okay. I guess I'll see you later."

Tobias moved toward the man who stood, caught like an animal. He put his arms on Aiden's shoulders. "May I give you a kiss goodbye?"

Aiden nodded once, twice. Tobias leaned in, and their lips met and Tobias knew—this could be it. Shit. He stepped back, and stared at the blue eyes for a moment. Aiden blinked, the long lashes covering the blue for just a moment. Just long enough for Tobias to want to see his eyes again.

"I'll walk you out." He moved down the hallway ahead of Aiden, his bare feet curling on the icy wooden floor. The long white walls leading to the stairway were hung with photographs of friends, architecture he loved, photos with his housemates, Freddie and Reece, but no boyfriends. He hadn't had one in a long time. He wondered if he could have one now.

They made their way down, and through the living room and its long green couch, fake leather chairs, television cabinet, and one bookcase-lined wall. Tobias didn't want to open the oiled, dark wooden panel of the front door. He didn't want to let the day intrude. Despite Aiden saying he could text him, he had a feeling the man wanted nothing more than to run. But he opened the door anyway.

It's what men did. They let people go when they wanted to leave.

"Thanks. Um, I had a nice time." Aiden ducked his head.

"I did too, I really did. I'll talk to you later."

"Yeah, catch you later."

And Tobias watched as he hurried down the steps toward the bus stop on the corner. He *really* hoped he'd see Aiden again.

And, not wanting to face his housemates, he rushed upstairs, hoping to duck into his bedroom before whoever was in the bathroom emerged.

He would have to confront them, and soon, but not this morning.

8

AIDEN

Wow, the temperature really had dropped. It was freezing, literally freezing. Aiden stepped carefully over frozen patches of ice from recent rains that had turned solid underfoot. His boots crunched and scraped as he hurried from the communal house he lived in, situated three blocks from the soup kitchen. He hunched under his wool hat, the hood of his coat pulled up, scarf tied tight around his neck.

The neighborhood was on the edges of the industrial section near the river, not quite in among the warehouses, but close enough. Traffic wound down the street, commuters heading for the Hawthorne Bridge, which would take them downtown.

He still couldn't believe he'd gone home with that guy last night. Tobias. Unbelievable. How in the world had he let that happen? First whatever that weird thing was in the church, which was a little fuzzy in his mind this morning, then too many beers bought by a man with beautiful brown eyes. Next thing he knew, he was waking up in a stranger's bed.

"Whoooh," he exhaled. *What is up with you man?* He could still feel the burn of Tobias's lips on his, and the warmth in his heart from whatever had happened with that piece of stained glass. St. Brigid. He shook his head. No time to ponder; he was already late for his shift.

The high wooden gate was already open when he arrived, that meant he was *really* late. He should have been in before opening to help make the tea, and get started with chopping the piles and mounds of vegetables that would make up today's soup—turkey barley, always a crowd pleaser.

Some guests huddled on the benches outside, among the wintering container garden. They sipped at steaming cups of tea. Most of the guests were gathered under the overhang that sheltered the outdoor seating area, sitting closely together, trying to keep warm. If he'd been here at the start, he would already have opened up the big brick dining room and let people come in. He'd talk to the crew chief about it.

Aiden raised his hand in greeting and got a few "good mornings" in reply.

He slammed through the metal doors to the old brick dining room, sparing a glance for the overcrowded altar, with its giant statue of Our Lady of Guadalupe, a cross, a Buddha, and assortment of other religious icons and objects. Despite them being a Catholic Worker, they wanted to welcome everyone, so the altar was a home to every religion, just as the kitchen tried to be a home to everyone who walked through the doors.

People were moving slowly behind the counter, and the usual banter wasn't happening. Even the radio was off. That was strange. He took off his hood and his wool cap and started unwinding his scarf. Stingray came toward him, with a stricken look on her face. Her mouth was tight and there were extra lines around her eyes.

"You're late today," she said. No mention of the fact that she hadn't seen him at the house this morning.

"Yeah, sorry I got caught up. Is everything okay? People seem weird."

"People *are* weird," she replied.

He took his coat off and went to hang it up in the closet behind the kitchen. She followed behind. "I need to tell you something."

He stopped midway, arm reaching for a hanger. "What? What happened?"

"Hang up your coat, I'll get you a cup of tea."

Now he felt worried. There was a tension in his stomach, his belly was tight, his throat was tight. Whatever was going on, it wasn't good, he could feel it. Aiden followed Stingray into the tiny break room with its sad wall of old beat-up metal lockers and a long table filled with donated baked goods. The coffeepot still hadn't been cleaned from yesterday; there was dark sludge at the bottom.

"Sit down," she said. They both sat in a couple of old pressed plastic chairs with wobbly metal legs. Everything felt wobbly. As if the whole world was slightly off kilter.

"Would you please just tell me what's happened?"

She looked at him stricken, her eyes suddenly a hundred years old. "It's Mary Jo."

He grew very still. "Mary Jo? I just saw her. She was just in yesterday. I sat with her before the cops came in."

"She froze to death last night."

"What? That's impossible, I thought she was inside?"

Stingray shook her head. "No. Her ex beat her up. She ended up back on the street."

"She didn't say anything." But she did have those bruises

all over her face. Damn it. Maybe he should have pressed her on it.

"Yeah, well, apparently they had a big blowup two nights ago and she was sleeping rough last night when the cold snap came."

"I don't understand. She just... She's *dead*?"

"Apparently the hypothermia came on quick. At least that's what the paramedics said."

"What are we going to do? I mean, does she have family? She has family, right? She's talked about a sister?"

"Back in Texas. We're trying to contact them."

"Oh man."

"I know this is a lot to take in, and I also know that we have a lot of work to do still to get lunch prepped. Take a couple minutes, though." Stingray squeezed his shoulder and walked out of the break room.

Aiden collapsed backward on the chair, clutching his chest; his heart was beating too fast and he felt that fire again. That crazy flame. It felt as though it was going to engulf him.

"Why?" he said. "Why does this shit keep happening? I don't understand it."

He looked around the break room, at the day-old muffins, the sludge in the coffeepot, the short bookcase filled with paperback donations. He loved this place, but right now it looked bleak. It wasn't a home, like they all tried to pretend it was. It wasn't even a safe haven. It was just a bandage, a fucked-up, ineffective, bandage.

There was that anger again, ready to spike into fury if he let it. He couldn't let it. Looking down, he realized his hands were clenched, and slowly unfurled his fingers, stretching them wide. Then he exhaled.

Get a grip Aiden, you have to get to work, other people need you.

Other people *always* needed him. That was his job. That was the thing he had promised to God when De Porres House first took him in: that he would help. That he would always help.

Sighing, he stood up and started to walk back to the kitchen. It felt as though his boots were filled with lead, his bones ached, and the fire still burned in his chest. He hoped it really wasn't the sign of something worse, like a heart attack. He washed his hands at the little sink by the large dishwashing station, dried them carefully, and bent into the cabinet to drag out an apron. Just go through the motions. Get through the day.

"Hey man." It was Reggie, one of his community house-mates, brown face already shiny with sweat from scrubbing potatoes and hauling bags of onions. "You heard about Mary Jo?"

"Yeah man, I can't believe it." Aiden shook his head. "I just..." he raised his hands and then dropped them again.

"I know man. It sucks. Well, can you get a bag of carrots out? They still need to be scrubbed and chopped. Lupe's already working on the turkey."

"Yeah, I'll get the carrots started."

"Peace."

Aiden moved in slow motion toward the glass-fronted refrigerator filled with waxed boxes of lettuce, cabbage, carrots, and zucchini. He opened the door, dragged out a big box of carrots, turned the water on in the large industrial sink next to the one Reggie was working at, and dumped the orange root vegetables in. They thumped and rolled as the water cascaded down. Aiden rolled up his sleeves, picked up the scrub brush, and fought back tears.

"This isn't right," he muttered to the water. "This isn't right," he said louder, picking up a carrot and beginning to scrub at it, scrubbing away the dirt and the tiny small rootlets that looked like hairs. He threw the carrot into the next sink.

"People shouldn't have to die," he said. "People shouldn't have to die. Not like this. Not ever."

Reggie looked over from the next sink over. "I feel you, man."

NINE

I t felt good to be up in Raquel's attic, under the white peaked ceiling, preparing the altars, setting out the cushions, smelling the ghostly layers of incense from years of rituals. The space would always smell that way, he imagined, even if Raquel ever decided to move.

He couldn't imagine Raquel ever living anywhere else, but he supposed once Zion, her son, was grown, maybe she would.

The attic looked beautiful; it was clean and spare, with the white canted ceiling that angled down to knee walls holding some short bookcases and chests of drawers filled with ritual objects and altar cloths.

Since the encounter with his father had ensured that he was completely off his center, Tobias decided he would follow Brenda's advice. After Aiden left, and his housemates had taken off for work, Tobias had emerged from his room, eaten breakfast, then gone to his office to set things back to rights.

After he'd cleaned up the mess he'd left the day before,

he took himself back home and spent the afternoon going over the basics of his magical training.

He'd taken a ritual bath, gotten dressed again, lit a candle and sat in meditation, revisiting the same drills he'd first learned when he joined the Arrow and Crescent—centering, boundary work, the blade, the wand, the cup, the dish.

Finally, a sense of himself returned. He actually found his center again. From that place, he visited his sorrow. He felt the anger just beneath the tears. His sense of helplessness. His constant, ticking rage.

Then he started over. He picked up his blade, the tool of his will, and drank from the cup of wisdom. He remembered that he was a witch, dedicated to the Goddess Brigid. She of the forge, of poetry, and of healing. Tobias's special matron.

Tonight was Imbolc, Brigid's day, and he really hoped tonight's ritual was going to help.

Maybe in order to be healed, I need to be forged, he thought, as he combed the baskets of supplies on one of the low bookcases. There they were, a stack of creamy beeswax tapers, just where Raquel had said they would be. *Maybe in order to be strong enough...I need to set myself between the hammer and the anvil. Let the Goddess do what she will.*

He didn't want that, had never wanted it, but nonetheless, those words rang true inside. Maybe, just maybe, in order to truly heal, he had to give control over to something greater than himself.

Not that there wasn't still fear. The face of the Goddess as the metalworker, the forger, wasn't an aspect Tobias worked with much. Had he been running from it? Unwilling to go through the necessary process of softening, being hammered into shape, and then submitting himself to the shock of hardening again?

It seemed easier to remain either soft or hard. The thought of putting himself through the ordeal of becoming who he was only to make himself vulnerable again? What if he shattered? What if the Goddess couldn't put him back together again?

Through the open attic door, he heard the other coven members arriving downstairs, greeted by Raquel's son, Zion. That was a pretty special kid. Tobias wondered if he would join the coven someday. Raquel said he had to wait until he was fifteen to make that decision. Seemed wise.

Tobias looked around, making sure that there was a bright velvet or patchwork-patterned cushion for each coven member, set out in a more of an oval than a circle, given the length of the room.

He filled the great dark bowl that would represent Brigid's well with water from a pitcher, and checked to see that Epsom salts and alcohol were ready for the cauldron fire. And last? Arranging the nine beeswax tapers—one for each coven member—into a fan around the central pillar candle.

"Okay, that's it," he said, right as he heard footsteps on the stairs. Raquel poked her head in. She was a beautiful African American woman with waist-length dreadlocks and a brilliant smile. Her high cheekbones grew even more pronounced as she smiled at him.

"You ready, Tobias?"

"Yep. Everything's in order," he said.

"Okay," she exited again, he heard her saying something and the sound of a dozen footsteps followed.

Moss, a Japanese American man, gave him a hug and plopped bonelessly on the pillow to his right. He was an activist, and, being close to Tobias's age, it seemed like they'd hang out more often. But though Tobias liked Moss, he always seemed a little too intense. Selene, on the other hand, he loved. An eighteen-year-old artist, Selene was kind and wise beyond their years. Always elegant in their black clothing, with perfect ruby lips and winged eyeliner, Selene squeezed his arm and sat on his left.

The others smiled at him and took their places.

Tobias dropped his attention into the stillness in his belly, a place he imagined resting between his navel and his pelvis. He took three deep breaths and relaxed his forehead, relaxed his hands, relaxed his feet. Allowing his attention to travel outward, he tried to imagine the boundary around himself where his energy bled into Moss on his right and Selene on his left. They felt solid and liquid, each in turn.

Tobias smiled. Coven was family. Coven was home. If anything would help him, ritual would.

He felt movement. Tempest stepped forward, shimmering blade in her small, strong hand. The sides and back of her head were shorn close as usual, only a fall of hair from the top was long. This month, it was dyed a magenta red. Tobias closed his eyes again, deepening his breathing. He imagined the blue fire that had snaked its way from the double-sided blade, forming the sphere of protection, the sphere that delineated this place and time from ordinary place and time. The sphere that marked holy ground and sacred space.

He opened his eyes as he caught the scent of damp pine moving forward. Cassiel. She always smelled like a forest in the rain. He wondered if she knew that. Her brilliant red curls cascaded down her back tonight and she wore loose, black wool trousers, topped by a flowing white shirt.

Tobias could feel the energy of the sphere humming around his shoulders.

Cassie turned to the north and began to recite the cantrip that would call the Elements and seal the sphere. "By earth..." She turned, following the energy laid down by Tempest's blade. "By wind. By flame, by sea. By moon, by sun, by dusk, by dark, by witch's mark..."

He felt all the elements called in turn and felt the energy in the room begin to shift and deepen.

"We consecrate this holy ground, with sight, and sound, and breath twined 'round. With will and love, from below to above..." Cassiel swept her hands in an arc, then brought her palms together in front of her heart. "Let the magic portals open."

Tobias felt his spine straighten. It was as if every part of him, body and spirit, had aligned with the cosmos. He felt a sense of rightness for the first time in what seemed like weeks.

Raquel, Brenda, and Alejandro stepped forward then, to call on Brigid herself.

The three wove in and out among each other, tracing one another's footsteps, twining their voices.

"Exalted One!"

"Fiery Arrow!"

"Brigid of the green mantle, Brigid of the forge!"

"Lady of the healing waters, Keeper of the flame!"

They raised their arms to the peaked, white-painted ceiling. Tobias lifted his own arms, calling the Goddess in his heart.

"Come to us!"

"Be with us!"

"Shape us! Inspire us! Make us whole!"

Then the whole coven began to chant. "Sacred well and

rising fire, kindle now our soul's desire! Sacred well and rising fire, kindle now our soul's desire!"

They chanted and chanted, words and breath rising with the candle flames, building power in the attic room, until the air was thick with it.

"She is here," Raquel announced.

"Blessed be," Alejandro and Brenda replied.

Tobias could feel dampness on his cheeks. It had been a week of tears. Tears were cleansing, the coven had taught him.

He didn't like to cry; he'd been trained, quite brutally, not to. But as a healer, he knew that sometimes tears were the only way through. For other people. And maybe now, for him. *Shit.* He swiped at his face and took a shuddering breath.

One by one, each coven member stepped forward and dipped their hands into the water of the well and swiped a palm across the blue flame of Epsom salts and alcohol fire that danced in the cauldron. Then each person picked up a beeswax taper. The scent of the fragrant wax increased as the room heated with the fire from the cauldron and the heat of their bodies. Every person said a prayer and made a pledge, then lit their candle from the large central pillar candle that Alejandro ignited from the cauldron itself.

And then it was Tobias's turn. His mouth grew dry, any shreds of peace inside his soul having fled. He knew that Brigid could be harsh, like Brenda. Like Raquel. *Like healing*, he thought.

He knew it wasn't always easy, but that didn't make him feel less afraid. He stepped forward anyway, taking a deep breath, and then sank to his knees on the carpet in front of the cauldron and the well.

"Holy Brigid," he said, kneeling in front of the altar,

"help me to know what I must do, help me in my work. Help me to find the next turning on my path. Triple-faced Goddess, forge me. Make me strong. Then show me the way."

He breathed deeply, and blessed himself with the waters of the well, and passed his palm over the flames of the cauldron, feeling the heat just touch his skin.

I don't know what to pledge, he thought. His prayer had come fairly easily, but the promise? His mind was empty as he gazed into the flames. "Brigid help me."

:Forge the fires of justice within the fires of love.: The voice rang through his head like a hammer striking a sword upon an anvil. Sharp and bright, it rang through his whole being. He felt filled with sound, with fire, with water. *But how?* he thought. And really? Love?

:Love is the strongest force in the world,: the voice said. *:Stronger than anger, fear, or hate. Just speak the words, my child. Speak the words.:*

The voice echoed in his mind. He didn't know what the words meant yet; he just knew he had to say the words aloud to seal his fate, to seal his pledge, to make good on whatever it was he was promising. He just hoped it wasn't going to bring disaster. He hoped it wouldn't kill him.

"Oh, stop being dramatic," he muttered. He took another deep breath and said out loud in front of the eight members in his coven, "I will forge justice within the fires of love."

Then he lit his beeswax taper from the central flame and moved back to take his place within the circle.

10

AIDEN

Aiden walked like a man with a purpose. Wool cap tucked over his ears, long underwear on beneath his heavy work pants. Boots. And the ever-present waterproof winter jacket over it all. His chin was covered with the ubiquitous long navy scarf wound one hundred times around his neck. He carried two medium-sized pieces of cardboard tucked beneath his left arm.

He walked past houseless folks gathered in clumps on the sidewalk. He strode past shops and coffee kiosks, restaurants and the taller buildings that held who knew what sorts of corporate offices. There were people everywhere, all hurrying to get somewhere warmer than these downtown city streets.

Working the soup kitchen that day had been really hard. Everyone was upset about Mary Jo, including all the guests, of course. People were grieving. A lot of tears went into the giant soup pots. A couple of fights broke out in the yard, but luckily those were pretty quickly diffused.

The fact that any one of them could die at any moment was a bleak reminder of just how hard the day-to-day was when you didn't have a house to call a home. The world was against these people, including nature itself, it seemed.

Times like these, Aiden wished he could fix the whole world.

"What would you fix it to?" Reggie would ask.

Aiden didn't have an answer to that question. So he just kept showing up.

Some of the kitchen workers were planning Mary Jo's memorial and had invited Aiden to stay after shift. He couldn't do it.

Everything was still roiling inside of him—her death, his intermittent fury, that weird fire that still burned in his chest...and his confusion over Tobias. He was *really* attracted to the man, but there was something strange about him. He had all that stuff on the dresser in his room. It looked like an altar, but it had some pretty strange looking things on it. Like a knife. What was *that* about?

But there wasn't time to dwell on it right now.

The only thing that Aiden felt clear about was what he was about to do. *That* was the thing that should have been taking up his attention.

It was still cold, icy even, and clouds were gathering overhead again. He couldn't tell if it was for snow or for rain. All he knew was the fire in his heart was guiding him. Maybe it was St. Brigid. Maybe it was his own certainty. Maybe it was even foolishness. It didn't matter. What mattered was, he was carrying a piece of cardboard downtown and he was going to kneel in front of the police station, and he was going to remain there as everyone got off work and walked past by him. And he was going to pray.

It was the one thing he knew: out of all of his confusion, he could pray.

He approached the station, a fortress of grayish-tan slabs

of concrete, with a two large safety-glass windows flanking wide glass doors crowned with concrete that framed in three other windows forming an arch. The building itself rose up in a tall promontory to the darkening skies, the only relief being a strange concave sweep of mirrored windows in the middle.

There were no welcoming steps. No broad sidewalks on which people could congregate. The City of Portland Police Bureau was not a place to rest one's bones or chat with a friend. It was a place you came only when you had business there, willing or not.

Some officers hurried in and out of the big, glass doors. People passed by, mostly office workers, heading to the buses or street cars that would take them home. Aiden ignored them. He wanted just the right spot. A spot that wouldn't get him moved along too quickly, but a spot where everyone who walked by or through those doors would see him. It was going to be tough. The sidewalk was broad enough for two or three people to walk abreast, but not so broad that he couldn't be seen as an obstruction.

Oh well. So be it.

He doubled over one of the pieces of cardboard under his arm and set it on the sidewalk closest to the building entrance and knelt down. Good. Plenty of space for a wheelchair user to get by him if they needed to.

The second piece of cardboard read—*"Houseless people shouldn't have to die. I pray for the city of Portland."* He propped that onto his thighs, turned his gloved palms upward to the clouds, bowed his head, and began to pray.

As he prayed, a slight wind came up, threatening to take his cardboard sign away. He clutched at the edges with the fingers of both hands. He could sense some people pausing as they walked by, reading his sign.

"Amen man," a deep voice said.

"You should go home," said another. "Leave the police alone, it's not their fault."

He didn't care. He didn't care what anyone said. The fire in his heart had told him to come and pray.

Despite all of Aiden's layers, the cold settled in fast. It still wasn't as bad as houseless people had it. They slept in this every night. They wandered around in this every day, saving enough coins to sit in a coffee shop for a while, if the coffee shop would even let them. Sitting through sermons at the rescue missions that insisted if people wanted to get fed they had to hear the word of God. Riding buses from the beginning to the end of the line. Some of them turned to prostitution or petty thievery as their best choices for survival.

It was so clear to him now, all the things he hadn't seen growing up as a pretty solidly middle-class child. A lot of the things that his parents said were bad, some people didn't have much of a choice around. They didn't have much of a choice because the world was set up against them.

There was pain in the world, and there was suffering, and "That suffering is caused by greed," he said out loud.

"And that suffering is caused by avoidance," he continued. "And that suffering is caused by lack of attention and lack of care. Don't we see?" he asked, opening his eyes. He stared at the traffic going by, at the people walking. "Can't we see, we need to rebuild this world? Can't we see that *your* pain is *their* pain is *our* pain? Can't we see?"

A few people stopped to listen for a while, then shook their heads and walked on. His heart was aching now, burning. The image of St. Brigid rose up in his head, her stained glass eyes staring down at him.

"Holy Brigid, I don't really know who you are, but you

seem to know who I am and I don't really know what I'm doing, but I need you to help me." A warmth suffused his body and a sense of calm surrounded him, as if someone had wrapped a warm shawl across his shoulders. He shuddered, and then inhaled and sank back into prayer.

He would be here for as long as it took. For as many days as were needed.

11

TOBIAS

The coven was in the big Unitarian church downtown. It was a beautiful old brick church with a large Black Lives Matter banner hanging outside.

Tobias actually loved the sanctuary of this church. But that wasn't where they were tonight. They were in one of the big meeting rooms in the more recently built center off the main church. The room was a regular utilitarian space, white walls, a dry erase board, and stackable, gray padded chairs.

The room was full, with maybe fifty or sixty people gathered, facing the front of the room where a couple of couple of facilitators sat conferring with each other.

"You see them staring at us?" Raquel said. She did not look happy. The whole coven was jammed into the back of the room, just inside the door, looking for places to sit. Even the coven members who hadn't yet unzipped their coats didn't quite look run of the mill. Selene, in their Goth wear. Moss, in his anarchist black. Brenda, in her flowing skirts... None of them was ordinary.

"Yeah," Tobias responded. "Think they're not happy with our pentacles?"

"Screw them," she murmured. "We have just as much right to be here as the Baptists. Besides, we were invited."

Tobias scowled, "Yep. Well, a lot of religious people have trouble with witches, I guess it's to be expected."

Moss interjected, "Come on, it's twenty-seventeen, this is Portland, Oregon. I mean it's not like we're in the middle of Podunk-nowhere and no one's even heard of witchcraft."

"Yeah, well, *hearing* about witchcraft and having to deal with witches at your interfaith meeting are two different things, I guess," Tobias replied. "Let's try to get seats before they're all gone."

They squeezed past some of those aforementioned Baptists. Tobias made sure to smile broadly at them. He got a couple of timid smiles in response. The rest of the people looked away. Oh well, their loss.

The pastor of the Unitarian Church had invited the Arrow and Crescent Coven specifically.

"We need to shake this interfaith group up," he had said. "There are too many complacent people, too many people who think interfaith means Baptists, Presbyterians, a Unitarian, and a Catholic. Oh, and if we're lucky, maybe a Jew."

Yeah, looking around, Tobias saw what looked to be a couple of rabbis at least, and maybe some Buddhists, though he wasn't sure. Probably no Hindus, and certainly no Sikhs. Tobias wondered if the coven could work on that. Do some actual outreach, or talk to the pastor about it, at any rate. There weren't even any first nations folks present, that he could tell.

He wondered if anyone on the Interfaith Council had contact with any of the Multnomah or Wasco peoples. Even if the tribal members were Christian, they would add a much-needed viewpoint to the group.

One step at a time, he thought to himself. The witches were here now. The Sikhs and others would hopefully come later. If it turned out to be worth it.

More people crowded into the room.

"I guess we should have gotten the sanctuary after all," said a brown-skinned Black woman with slicked-back hair. She was dressed like a business woman, in a skirt and pumps. Tobias thought she was with the Unitarians, though he wasn't sure. She was acting like a meeting facilitator.

"Well, it's too late now," she said, and raised her voice. "Please just try to find a spot. I'm afraid some of you will have to stand, so we'll try to make tonight's meeting short."

People shuffled around, excusing themselves and shucking out of their heavy coats. The room was already warm. Tobias felt some sweat on his upper lip. He swiped at it.

"What time is this meeting supposed to start?" he asked Brenda. He was sandwiched between Brenda and Raquel.

"I think 6:30," she said, "I don't know."

"And *how* long is it going to run?"

"These sorts of meetings?" she said, "Despite what Jaqueline just said, they always run too long. You can duck out if you need to."

He settled himself into the chair, his heavy coat on his lap. Waiting. And then *he* walked through the open door— Aiden. Tobias's heart thumped faster. He licked his lips. Wow, the man was beautiful.

Tobias stared at Aiden as he walked to the front, dark hair swept off his pale brow, and those long, dark eyelashes framing his eyes. He was still wrapped up in his heavy winter coat with a navy scarf around his neck, and a wool cap tucked inside his hands. He must have felt Tobias looking at him, because he looked up, startled, and stared across the room.

Giving Tobias a quick nod and a small smile, he turned to the facilitator who had just spoken. Tobias felt relieved. The smile signaled that Aiden must have meant it about having another date sometime. At least he hoped so.

Aiden sat down in a chair in the front. That same facilitator stood up again.

"Okay everybody, thank you all for coming. I know it's a cold night but it's only going to get colder and at least we have a warm place to meet in. My name is Jaqueline, and I'm with the Unitarian Universalist congregation and will be facilitating this meeting tonight. I invite Rabbi Schwartz to please come up and lead us in an opening prayer."

Rabbi Schwartz was a tall, thin woman with a skullcap on her head, glasses, and short gray-and-black hair curling around her face. She wore a purple shirt and black jeans.

"Thank you, Jaqueline," she said, then addressed the gathering, "You can close your eyes or leave them open, whatever works for your tradition."

And she raised her hands and closed her own eyes.

"I call upon the spirit of love to enter this space. I call upon the spirit of understanding to be with us. May we seek your guidance. May we open our minds and hearts. Please give us the strength to help our brothers and sisters on the streets during these cold months when they need us the most. May we shine the light of love for them. May the light of love fill each of us and guide our words and our thoughts during this meeting, Amen,"

"Amen," people replied.

"Blessed be," said several coven members.

"Blessed be," Tobias said.

The facilitator stood again and said, "Thank you, Rabbi" as the rabbi made her way back to her seat. "I'd like to ask Aiden from De Porres house to speak to us, and then afterwards we'll break into small groups to start brainstorming ideas for our winter task force. Just feeding people isn't enough. We need to put pressure on the city to actually do something to solve the problem of homelessness in Portland. And I know you're all here because you're deeply concerned and interested in this. It's time, though, that we move towards real action. So let's figure that out, folks. But first, Aiden."

He stood, wearing a simple navy button down shirt over a white T-shirt. His face looked cold and drawn. Tobias sat up straighter in his chair, waiting. Aiden closed his eyes and took in a deep breath. Tobias breathed in with him.

Eyes still closed, Aiden spoke, voice reaching clearly to the back of the room.

"Mary Jo died last night. She died cold and alone. She died on a sidewalk in this city wrapped in a sleeping bag. Damp. Lonely. I hope she fell asleep and didn't know she was dying. I hope she had some comfort in the end."

His eyes snapped open. "But I don't know that she did. I know that this city did not give her enough comfort. I know that this city did not offer enough help. Our kitchen fed her every day and offered tea and conversation, but we couldn't offer her a real home. Her home was among the other people on the streets who are also struggling. This city is responsible for each of them. We are responsible for each of them and we are responsible for the life and death of Mary Jo."

He closed his eyes again, mouth pinched, face even paler than before. Then, like the rabbi before him, he lifted his hands. His blue eyes snapped open once again, his gaze moving around the room.

"I spent this afternoon kneeling in prayer in front of the police station. As you know, the police have been making sweeps of the homeless camps, or as we call them, the houseless camps. These camps provide shelter, home, a place to live in community, but they are consistently threatened by people whose homes happen to be houses instead of clustered tents. The more those camps get dispersed, the more those homes are scattered, the more people like Mary Jo will die from cold, from neglect, from want."

Tobias's stomach churned with sour bile. Regret and a sense of guilt twined with grief. He wasn't sure how many of those emotions were his own. He wasn't usually an empath, but Aiden affected him in ways he wasn't used to.

"We have got to stand together and stop the sweeps, and find a better way to show these people that we are part of their community. And my prayer today was that we each be filled with the holy fire. The fire of change. The fire of justice. The fire of love. And I prayed for that fire to move through us, kindling in us that desire to step forward and be a presence of hope and true justice, not just charity."

He looked around the room again. "I know many of you are very involved in charity. So am I. The works of mercy are important. Well, I understand now, maybe for the first time in my life, that the works of mercy are not enough. We need to figure out together what the works of justice are, and I know in my heart that is the work of this group. It is our holy work."

Tobias felt as though breath barely flowed into this lungs. The air around him was practically vibrating. The room was hushed, the air felt thick. Tobias felt the pressure of it on his face and his chest.

"Jaqueline asked us to form task forces to make real change here," Aiden said. "The first thing I ask us to do is to insist that the police stop the sweeps. The other ideas I'm going to leave up to you. Thank you."

Aiden lowered his hands then, and the air rushed back into Tobias's lungs.

"Powerful," Raquel murmured next to him.

Tobias nodded, "Yes."

Damn. The world seemed determined to turn every emotion in his life on its head, didn't it? Because Tobias knew right then, in that moment, that he was in love.

12

AIDEN

Aiden felt as though his skin were vibrating. He couldn't even look up. He collapsed into his chair, trying to slow his breathing down, one hand clutching his heart, sure that he was going to burn up, burn alive.

"Do you need anything, Aiden?" Jaqueline asked as she crouched near his chair, slim skirt tucked behind her knees. Her brow was creased, though the rest of her face looked perfect beneath the slick coif of her hair.

So many people looked out for him, he realized. Usually it was Stingray. She was always attuned to what her crew was doing, and how they were feeling. Plus, she'd been one of the people who had lobbied to the community to take Aiden in when he had first arrived, a hungry, scared seventeen-year-old.

Jaqueline was nothing like Stingray on one hand, but the two women shared some characteristics. Both of them were strong, not afraid to fight, and as nurturing as the day was long.

He looked up. "No, no, I'm okay. I just need to sit for a moment."

"You let me know. I'm going to get the groups started. Okay?"

"Sounds great," he said.

Okay, Aiden, what's happening? He wondered if he shouldn't have gone to the doctor like the priest had asked him to, except this didn't actually feel physical, despite the weird physical manifestation of it. It felt—he wasn't sure —*meta*physical, spiritual.

What are you, some kind of holy man? He scoffed at himself, shaking his head. He didn't feel like any kind of holy man, but they were the only people who had these weird experiences, in his mind. They were the only ones that people told these kind of stories about. That was so not what he needed. Going out to gay bars, picking up strange men, waking up in their beds and then what? Being a holy man? They didn't seem to go together.

And Tobias was here. Of all the places...and it looked like he was with those witches Aiden had heard some of the more conservative Baptists grumbling in the hallway.

A coven had walked into the Portland Interfaith Council. It was like a bad joke. Who'd have thought that would even happen? Aiden had barely been able to look at Tobias when he was standing up talking. His eyes kept glancing over that sharply chiseled face, the long nose, the deep brown eyes, the full lips.

He couldn't deny the attraction. He was a metal filing and Tobias was a magnet.

"Just stop it," he muttered, head in his hands. If he could just sit here and breathe awhile, maybe Tobias would end up in a group trying to plot some help for the houseless of Portland and Aiden could make his excuses to Jaqueline and slip away. He wanted another date with the man, sure, but he wasn't quite ready for Tobias to have seen him like this, with the fire pouring through him.

And if it turned out he was a witch? What then?

He felt overwhelmed now. Exposed. Confused.

"Aiden."

It was that voice, sweet honey in a cup of warm and soothing tea. And the smell of him, like fire igniting charcoal and the first hiss of frankincense, smoke wafting towards the sky. He smelled like comfort, and like a place of worship, both. Aiden breathed in and finally lifted his hands from his face and sat up again.

Tobias crouched down in front of him. "Are you okay? You look kind of ill. Do you need me to get you some water?"

"No, thanks. I think I'll be fine." As if.

Tobias pulled a chair up next to him. He held out a woven, equal-armed cross that looked like it was made out of straw. Aiden grew still inside when he recognized it. It was the cross from the stained glass window. He looked up into the brown eyes he'd spent hours staring into two nights before. "The cross of St. Brigid," he said.

"Yes. I've been weaving them all week. We just celebrated her holiday—Imbolc, the Irish call it. The coven always gets together to honor her. Actually, I honor her every day. I say my prayers, light my candles"—he nodded —"you know, magic stuff."

Aiden's stomach clenched. "Coven? You're in a coven?"

"Yes. Is that a problem?"

Aiden didn't know what to say to that. Of course it was a problem. Damn it. *Really, God? This is who you send me?*

Aiden didn't answer Tobias's question. "Magic stuff? Sounds more like Catholic stuff."

"Well," Tobias responded, smile not leaving his face, "I don't know how much you know about it all, but sometimes I think they're pretty much the same. Magic and...whatever Catholics do. And yeah, I'm here with my coven. Arrow and Crescent. And yes, before you get there, I call myself a witch."

Aiden shook his head.

Tobias held the cross out towards him. "I'd like you to have it," he said. Aiden reached for it, feeling the smooth, dry, papery quality of the straw, running his fingers over the bumps where other pieces of straw had been wrapped around the ends, tying off the arms of the cross. It looked like a pinwheel. Like the toy he had when he was eight. He loved running around with it as it blew in the wind, making whirring and clicking noises, colors flashing and flying as he ran.

"It's like a pinwheel," he said.

Tobias nodded. "Same basic principle. Every culture has a sun-wheel. This is the Irish form. We consider the equal armed cross to represent the seasons and the elements."

"Just looks like a cross to me," Aiden said.

Tobias nodded and sat back. He didn't say anything else, he just looked. Aiden felt that gaze on his skin, he felt his body respond. Witch or not, Tobias was the first person he'd been attracted to since he was, oh, gosh, sixteen probably. For years he'd hidden himself away, first just running, trying to find a home, and then working. The soup kitchen took up every ounce of him. He rubbed his chest again.

"Are you sure you're okay?" Tobias asked.

Aiden paused. If anyone understood weird stuff like this, it would be a witch, right? "I had a weird experience the other day and it's staying with me."

He could hear the murmur of people's voices as the small groups started up, discussing strategies. He heard

Mary Jo's name and felt the wave of grief crash through him again. Water meeting fire.

"What kind of experience?" Tobias asked.

Somehow, Aiden knew this man, this witch, would understand.

"I... It was weird. I was praying in church and nothing was happening, and I stopped in front of a stained glass window on my way out." He held up the straw cross. "St. Brigid, actually. And then all of a sudden, it felt like my heart was on fire and I collapsed. I came to with this priest standing over me, and my chest still burning."

"Was it a heart attack?"

"That's just it, no. Like, it wasn't that kind of classic pressure, left arm going numb thing. Besides, I'm too young and I'm healthy; I've never had a problem in my life. Got checked up at the clinic six months ago," he said. "It felt... spiritual. Do you understand that?"

"I do. And if you're willing to talk to a bunch of witches, I think Brenda or Raquel could help you out, or maybe Tempest. Tempest is a healer."

"Like you," Aiden said.

Tobias nodded. "Like me, but different skill set. And Brenda and Raquel, well, they're two of the wisest women I know."

"I don't know, Tobias. To be honest, I'm kind of freaked out by this whole witchcraft thing. It's news to me, you know. You could have told me."

"While we were dancing? When you kissed me? After the second beer? When exactly was the right moment, Aiden?" His voice sounded irritated. "You didn't tell me too much about yourself, either."

Then Tobias took a breath and looked around, as if he was searching for an answer somewhere among the groups of people gathered in clumps throughout the small room.

Aiden watched him, torn between wanting to curl up in the man's arms again, and run as far and fast as his boots would take him.

Tobias leaned forward and dropped his voice. "It's not a big deal. Think of it this way. Think of it as the religions people had before Jesus came. Think of it as the religion that people had when they just trying to get along with the land and the animals and just discovering how to use fire. Think of it that way. I mean, haven't you ever walked down the street and felt like the world was alive?"

"Yeah," Aiden said, "I guess I feel that sometimes. With the trees, or the people who come to eat at the kitchen. The priest calls that the indwelling spirit."

"Yes! That indwelling spirit is something witches work with all the time. We believe the world is alive: every plant, every rock, every drop of water, every flame, every person. We also work with Gods and Goddesses, those larger forces. Some of us feel that they make up that thing that you call God. Some of us feel they're all separate individual entities."

"And you?" Aiden said.

Tobias grinned. "Well, the jury's still out for me. But I work with Brigid a lot and I feel like she listens to me, and I feel like she helps me heal people. So as far as I'm concerned, Brigid at least is real, as real as anything else, as real as you sitting here." Then he laughed. Aiden liked his laugh a lot.

"What's so funny?" Aiden said.

"I didn't come to this meeting expecting to talk theology with you. I didn't expect to see you here at all. I suppose I should join a group, and figure out what we're going to do."

"Join my group," Aiden said, then flushed a little with

the boldness of that statement. "I mean, I really want to get people together to stop the sweeps. These people here, they'll join us if we come up with a plan. But mostly they're going to try to figure out more conservative ways to deal with the problem."

"And you want a more radical solution?" Tobias said.

"I just told you, man. My *heart's* on fire. I have to *grasp* something. I have to grasp the torch, I have to grasp the root. I don't know if any of this makes any sense. It doesn't really make sense to me, but all I know is I'm ready to do something drastic."

Tobias held out his hand. Aiden looked from the hand up to Tobias's face, then he nodded, transferred the Brigid's cross to his left hand, and took Tobias's right hand in his own. They shook.

Aiden found that he didn't really want to let go.

"I'm in," Tobias said. "Whatever you need, I'll do my best."

"Okay, I'll count on it."

But why did Tobias have to be a witch?

13

TOBIAS

All he wanted to do after the weirdly tense interfaith meeting was to take a shower, put on some sweatpants, and crawl into bed with a book. The meeting had turned into a session with Aiden where they alternately planned ways to gain justice for every homeless camp in Portland and Aiden asking him nervous questions about the craft.

At least he'd gotten another kiss out of the man before they parted ways. Tobias grinned at the memory of it as he slipped his key into the retro lock on the heavy front door. When he saw what was inside, he stifled a groan. His housemates.

Oh great. Just what he didn't want.

As soon as he stepped through the door, there they were, sitting on the green couch, smoking marijuana, eating what looked like a pint of mint chip ice cream, and watching *Doctor Who*. As usual.

Tobias so hadn't planned on dealing with this situation now, but he knew he shouldn't put it off, either. He stopped, dropped his messenger bag on the floor, and unbuttoned his coat.

"Hey, Tobias!" Freddie said, not taking his eyes from the flat screen.

Tobias just stood there, waiting for his housemates to turn their heads. Peter Capaldi was too engrossing. They cackled at some dinosaurs doing Goddess-knew-what on the screen. Tobias thought science fiction was about the future, so he had no clue what dinosaurs were doing on the stupid show.

He finally realized they must think he was watching along with them. Tobias couldn't stand around all night, waiting for two stoned people to figure out otherwise.

"When were you going to tell me about the deal?" he finally said.

"What are you talking about, dude?" Freddie asked, glancing his way, and delicately tamping out the blunt into an ashtray.

"Can you turn that off for a second?" Tobias asked. Reece grabbed the remote and paused the show. Tobias could tell she wasn't happy about having her cozy, lazy night interrupted. Well, tough shit.

Tobias squared off between the television cabinet and the sofa. "The deal you made with my *father*, asshole. To get what turns out is a pretty sweet deal on this house."

A deal he should have known was too good to be true in this rental climate. So much for his business being in the black. Damn it. How was he going to pay a rent increase here, and for his office space? He shouldn't have scheduled with Dr. Greene. No way was he going to be able to afford therapy. Not without a serious miracle.

Reece paused, a spoon loaded with ice cream half way to

her mouth. "Shit," she said. "I told you we should have said something."

"Shut up, Reece," Freddie snapped.

She dropped the spoon into the pint carton and smacked his bicep.

"No, Reece, don't shut up," Tobias said. "Tell me all about it. Tell me about how the two of you colluded with my snake of a father and didn't bother to let me know."

"It's just cheap rent, Tobias. What's so wrong about that?" Freddie replied. "I figured your dad just wanted to give you a present without you knowing about it."

Tobias dropped into one of the black, fake-leather armchairs across the coffee table, angled between the TV cabinet and the bookcase. He held his head in his hands for a moment, trying to get his anger under control.

He sat up. Freddie flinched. Good.

"You know I barely talk to my father. You knew I would never agree to this. Isn't that right?" He kept his voice low, even. His fingers gripped the bonded faux-leather chair arms.

"We're not going to lose the place, are we?" Reece asked.

It was a reasonable question, Tobias supposed. He clenched his molars.

"Well, my father is certainly going to raise our rent, now, isn't he? Now that he knows he can't manipulate me back into the life he wants."

Tobias stood again. "What the hell were you *thinking* Freddie? Men like my father never give anything away for free. They don't give *gifts*, they issue *promissory notes!* And this is one I never even got a chance to sign off on."

"Dude. I don't even know what you're talking about."

No, Freddie wouldn't. He'd quit his MBA at Reed because

it was too boring, and joined his own dad's investment firm where he did Goddess knew what. Reece was a perpetual student and wrote poetry. Mostly, they both just smoked pot.

But Tobias was the one without ambition.

"Sit back down," Freddie said. "We'll talk it out. I'm sure it'll all be fine. I can call my dad."

Tobias held up a hand. "Just...don't. Not right now. I'm going to call the Tenants Union sometime this week and see if we have a leg to stand on, which we probably don't, seeing as it's my *fucking family*. But I don't know that for sure. And whatever they say, we're going to do it."

He picked up his messenger bag and slung it over his shoulder. "And if we have to? We'll move."

"But..." Reece protested.

"I'm done with both of you for tonight. I just...can't. We'll talk more later."

Tobias walked up the stairs to his room. If he hadn't left, he might have been tempted to punch Freddie, and Freddie wasn't the one who deserved to be punched.

His father did.

Or maybe Tobias did, for being so stupid, and thinking everything was going to be all right if he just worked hard enough and believed.

Welcome to the real world, Tobias. Right. There was that. He could have been sleeping on the sidewalk, except given his background, it was highly unlikely. He didn't know what the statistics were that an educated, middle-class white guy would end up on the streets, but the odds still had to be leaning toward him being okay.

Didn't they?

Shutting his bedroom door, he looked around. He really liked this place. It felt like home. But if he had to leave it, he would. There was no way he would be any more beholden to his parents than he already was.

He hung his coat in the closet, dropped his boots to the floor, and flopped down on the bed.

Then he closed his eyes, body trembling from anger, and tried to slow his thoughts and emotions down enough to pray.

14

AIDEN

"Damn, it's still freezing," Stingray said. The bus bumped through the neighborhood, past bungalows and grocery stores. Aiden had to agree. The cold had settled in. It hadn't snowed since December and he hoped it wouldn't again. Rain was hard enough on houseless people. Snow? Almost impossible to deal with.

The inside of the bus smelled like damp wool and BBQ corn chips, and the skies were a brooding dark gray outside. They were en route to an encampment, hoping to make it there in time.

They'd been at the De Porres House kitchen when Stingray picked up the call. The cops were about to raid the big camp under the 205 freeway. People needed help.

There was a pretty big crew of volunteers that day, so Stingray left Reggie in charge, and called some folks at the community house for backup. Then she and Aiden grabbed their coats and they took off, catching the bus for the short ride from the industrial area near the river, where the kitchen was, to the more populated area of old working-class, southeast Portland.

"Thank you!" Stingray called out to the bus driver before swinging off the bus. It rumbled down the street, passing them by as they hurried the last few yards up to Foster Boulevard.

Cars whooshed by them, and the freeway roared as they approached, stinking of exhaust and cold winter air. Aiden could see the bright red and blue domes of some of the larger tents under the 205 overpass. This was one of the better established camps. It was in a great spot—out of the way, well protected by big boulders, a strange sort of dry-scaping the city had installed under the freeway, for what purpose, Aiden wasn't sure. As a consequence, you could barely even see the camp was there. It had been one of the nicer camps he'd visited. Well protected from the elements, it was cozy place for people to make a home.

"That's Ghatso's car!" Stingray said, pointing at a battered old Toyota parked nearby. Good. That meant the community house had rallied and some of the other kitchen workers were already there.

"I hope they're able to save the camp," Aiden replied.

Aiden was worried. He was still feeling strange, and Stingray had given him the option to be the one who stayed behind at De Porres House. But he knew he had to be out here; the fire inside him compelled him. Someone had to help these people.

Then he saw the white NorthWest Services truck. Damn it. That meant they were carting people's stuff away. It seemed like the cruelest punishment to people without a house, to take their few belongings. Even though they were supposed to be catalogued and saved for thirty days, if a person had nowhere to go in the interim, they were often turned into garbage, forcing people to start over, again and again.

The rage was back. It was a sourness, filling his chest and belly. His fists clenched inside his fingerless gloves. Over the noise of traffic, he heard shouting, and a woman screamed.

Stingray looked at him with wide eyes and broke into a trot. Aiden followed, boots striking the sidewalk. It felt good to run. The cold air singed his lungs, but the fire inside him wouldn't quit; it drew him towards the camp.

As they got closer, he could see between the boulders. It was a mess, a melee, NorthWest workers with their orange vests and white jumpsuits, and the cops in their dark uniforms, heavy, puffy, navy-blue winter jackets, struggling with houseless people over their meager belongings. Some people cried, others shouted. Some just stood, slumped with resignation.

He could see some of their community friends trying to intervene. Ghatso and Renee had placed themselves between some of the people and their tents, and the cops, but there just weren't enough of them to really help. One other De Porres community member, Brad, a tall, burly man with red hair poking out from his black watch cap, was screaming in a cop's face.

Aiden groaned. Who put Brad on negotiation? He was a firecracker, and never had a calm head. But in this situation, who could? Aiden found that he couldn't. He looked around, still trying to figure out what to do. How to help.

He turned to Stingray, who had stopped dead still. "What do we do?" he said. "There aren't enough of us."

"I don't know, but we can't just let this happen," she said. She ran over to Brad and put a hand on his arm. Aiden saw Brad jerk his arm away and turn his anger on her. She held up two placating hands, one towards Brad and one towards the cop. The cop looked like an immovable rock. He wondered if he even had a heart or brain. That was the rage talking, for sure.

He looked around in the confusion. There was so much movement happening everywhere. They needed a strategy, but it was too late for that. So what to do? He recognized some guests who ate at De Porres house regularly, packing up their stuff.

"Oh God, I hate this!" Aiden said. "What are we gonna do?"

Then he saw it, a tiny, skinny white woman in a ragged coat, the stuffing of her puffer jacket leaking out of holes, green cap askew on the top of her head. She was tugging on a tent, trying to pull it out of this one cop's hands as she screamed and cried. Aiden ran towards her. He started to help pull.

The cop yelled at him, "Get off!"

"Why are you taking her stuff?" Aiden yelled.

"Get off, sir. This is none of your business. We need to clear this camp."

"Why? It's freezing out. This is all these people have."

"They can go to a shelter."

"You know the shelters are full."

"They can go to a warming center."

He glanced at the woman. The tears were freezing on her face. "If she could go to a warming center, don't you think she would?"

He let go of the tent then, filled with a sudden, calm resolve. He walked around the tent and stood right in front of the cop.

"You need to leave these people alone."

"And you need to step back sir," the officer said. "We gave them twenty-four hours to clear, and they disregarded the order."

"Disregarded the order?" His throat was tight with trying not to scream in the cop's face. "You need to leave these people alone. This is their home. What if someone told you to leave *your* home? What would you do then, huh? Where would *you* go? What if you didn't have a fat savings account and a pension? Or a job? Or a family to take care of you? Where would you go then?"

Aiden took another step toward the man, who was broader and taller than he was, white face red with cold, green eyes flickering between anger and panic.

"I told you sir, you need to step back." The cop's hands were up, warning him away. Aiden stepped again. The cop shoved him, hitting his chest, hard. Aiden's arms wheeled out, grasping at nothing. There was only cold air.

He tried to catch himself but his boots hit a patch of ice on stone.

He heard his head crack on a rock, *Shit*, he thought, as he blacked out for the second time in a week.

15

TOBIAS

Tobias was in his office, Ibeyi on low, the two women's voices chanting devotional songs to the Orisha, in time with drums and synthesizers. The scent of fresh herbs wreathing his head was undercut by the sharp tang of the alcohol he used to make his tinctures. He was feeling a little more back in the groove this morning. The candles were still burning on his altar. He'd had quite a talk with Brigid this morning, asking for help.

He felt the power of her hammer, already pounding him into shape. He had no idea how that was going to turn out, but was attempting to let the process happen.

Meanwhile, he had work to do. He had clients to help, and he realized it didn't really matter how he felt about it. It was his work and the work needed to be done; people needed him even if he was angry, and sad, having a minor crisis of faith, and stuck between the hammer and the anvil of a Goddess he thought he knew, but had really just been avoiding.

So he was feeling okay. Not great, but okay. Well enough.

Tobias's hands were used to the work, used to picking

the proper herbs in the proper amounts, used to grinding them in his mortar and pestle. His body knew what his heart sometimes rejected. The herbs talked to his skin and bones, and to the energy that flowed around his body.

He particularly loved the feel of the wooden pestle in his hand and holding the mortar steady with his other, letting the scent rise as the leaves broke down and the oils were released. He really loved the tactility of this work—it grounded him. Since he tended to be so fiery—hot emotion, quick to seek change—working with the herbs made him slow down. It was kind of funny that he'd become an earth witch, instead of a fire witch. But Raquel said we always seek out balance, we seek out that which we need most to teach us, and the plants were that for him.

The music helped him focus. He let the the sound of drum and voice move through him as he worked. He couldn't help thinking of Aiden and that meeting. He still wondered what in the world he could do to help. That wasn't clear yet.

Aiden seemed to want him on his team, to actually go out and do physical protection. Tobias wasn't sure about that. Despite his emotional volatility, he'd always tried to keep out of trouble, and not step too far forward. It had been strange enough figuring out he was gay when he was eleven. He'd come to terms with it pretty quickly. But of course, not everyone around him did. He was lucky to have had some good friends, even to have a crush on a boyfriend or two. But still, he wasn't one of those people that shouted to the world who they were in a state of defiance. He knew that was an easy way to get killed.

But he'd defied his father anyway. He'd had to. It was either that, or lose his soul.

At any rate, here he was now, an adult, and successful

enough despite the added worry of not knowing if he was going to lose his home.

Despite his questions, he even had a purpose. Herbs and helping people were his purpose. His calling. But Tobias also wondered if there was something more. Talking with Aiden only increased his sense that he wasn't doing enough.

And the challenge from his parents to give it all away? To focus on nothing more than making money for other rich people? That was actually clarifying. That was not a way to forge justice from the fires of love. If he allowed his father to manipulate him back into being a good boy, he knew he'd lose it all. Coven. Aiden. Healing. Love. And whatever it was that Brigid was trying to teach him now.

He'd become just another cog in the machine designed to chew up people's lives and spit them out again.

His phone buzzed on the countertop. He looked at it— Aiden. He answered the phone.

"Hey Aiden, this is a nice surprise."

The man's voice was weak on the other end of the line. Barely audible. "Are you okay? I can barely hear you." Aiden spoke up and Tobias dropped the pestle from his right hand. It crunched against the St. John's Wort in the mortar. He was paying attention now. Oh no. It sounded bad. Really bad.

He glanced toward his altar. The candle flame in front of Brigid's cross flared upward and then died back down into a steady glow as he listened to Aiden's story. Aiden slurred his words slightly. Did he have a concussion?

"Did the cop hit you?" No. Shoved him. He'd hit his head on a stone. Tobias's fist clenched.

"Okay, I can come visit, and I'll bring you some herbs. Is there anything else you need? Soup or something? I don't know. What can I do for you?" Tobias grabbed a sheet of paper and scribbled down Aiden's address.

"I'll be there in thirty minutes, maybe forty minutes tops. Let me do a couple of things and get some get some herbs together and I'll be right there. Sit tight. Okay."

He set the phone down and exhaled, then turned to the altar again. He felt a flash of anger and worry. Walking to the altar, he picked up his athame, his double-sided, black-handled blade, and then his wand, a long, strong, dark piece of hawthorn, sanded and polished.

He held the symbols of fire and air in his hands for the first time in too long. Too many months. He realized then that all throughout the monthly coven meetings and rituals, and his prayers every morning, he hadn't really been doing the work of the *witch*. His afternoon before the Imbolc ritual notwithstanding, Brenda was right. He'd been neglecting his tools.

"No time like the present."

Aiden took in a deep breath, dropped his attention down and centered himself.

It was time to call his power back. *All* the way back. Holding the tools of will and intellect, the tools that cut, and the tools that formed boundaries, the tools that *chose*, he breathed in the feel of fire and breathed out the blessing of air.

He felt the earth of his body, and the water in his spit and the blood that raced through his veins, and he looked at the Brigid's cross and the cauldron, and the candle and the cup, and then he raised his head and said out loud: "I choose to know, I choose to act. I choose my power. My name is Tobias and I am a witch. And I pledge here in front of the elements of life and the Goddess Brigid herself that I will seek always the unfolding path of healing, of power, of fierce love and change. Brigid, on your special day you told me to forge justice from the fires of love. Teach me how. I vow to learn. I vow to do this work."

He raised the athame and the wand, arms forming a powerful vee shape in the air. "I, Tobias, will learn to the best of my ability to forge justice from the fires of love. Starting here, starting now. Beginning today. I will rise to the challenge in front of me. I set my feet on this path. I will follow my heart and do my will. Brigid arise! Brigid come! You are the lady of healing. You are the lady of inspiration. But you are also she who wields the hammer and forges the sword upon the anvil. Forge me. Shape me. Temper me. Make me strong and whole and ready for this work. So mote it be."

The energy around his body felt clear and strong for the first time in quite a while. Tobias could feel his aura shining around him like an egg of light. He nodded. It was good.

He kissed the blade and the wand, and he set them crossed in front of the candle on the altar. Then he took another breath and said, "Thank you for showing me the way." He extinguished the candle. "And whatever you need to hammer into me? Bring it on."

Tobias turned to his shelves of already-made tinctures and got to work blending them into a new formula. Aiden need him. And damn it, Tobias was going to show up.

16

AIDEN

Everything hurt.

His back, his head, his hands. Somehow, even his feet hurt. Aiden was tucked into the double bed in his room in the community house. It was a big, sprawling Victorian he shared with six other soup kitchen workers. He worked for room and board and a small stipend. He was grateful for the home.

His room was spare. Neat, like a monk's room. He had a quilt from home that his mother had mailed him once they figured out he was here to stay. It had been hand pieced by his grandmother in beautiful shades of green, burgundy, and blue. He loved the quilt. His grandmother had always been good to him.

The room smelled of the coffee and tea Renee and Brad were drinking. He tried to focus on Renee's face, but it hurt to have his eyes open at all. Renee had shut the burgundy curtains over his window so not too much light could come in. Not that there was that much light today anyway. It had warmed up enough for the rains to come, and he was grateful for the sound of it on the window.

The temperature was supposed to drop again tonight, bringing ice storms. Aiden felt for the people outside. He didn't know how most of them even survived; they made do, he knew. Houseless people were resourceful, if nothing else. He just wished they'd been able to save the camp under the freeway.

"I feel like I got cracked on the head for nothing."

"We're just lucky they didn't arrest us all," Renee said, perched on the chair near his bed. Brad and Renee were crowded into his room with cups of coffee and tea to give him a quick update. Stingray said she'd give them twenty minutes before she came back to shoo them out so he could rest.

Aiden supposed Renee was right. Apparently, Renee and Ghatso had dragged him off out of the way of the cops. The cops looked disgusted with them, Ghatso had said.

"They couldn't *bother* to arrest us." Brad said. He was standing hear the door. The room was too small for a second chair. "They just wanted us out of there. Wanted to prove their power."

Renee picked up the thread of complaint. "They didn't even need to deal with us. After you got knocked out, the cop that pushed you actually laughed. He wadded up that woman's tent and threw it in the back of the NorthWest Service truck."

"Bastards," Brad replied.

If Aiden's head hadn't felt as if an ice pick had been permanently affixed in the back of it, he would have shaken it.

Apparently, his comrades had somehow gotten him into the car, Brad and Renee carrying him, and gotten him to the hospital. Stingray and Ghatso had taken turns waking him up every two hours all night long. He was exhausted. But they said he was finally out of danger from the slight concussion.

He wondered whether or not he should press charges against the cop. Renee and Brad were split on that opinion too. Brad thought he should. Renee thought it might just get them all in more trouble. Aiden had no idea what to do, so he just lay here in bed, praying for the pain to go away.

There was a soft knock on the door. "Yes," he croaked. Brad cracked the door open, then turned and smiled.

"There's a Tobias here to see you. You feel up to more company?" Brad asked.

Tobias had actually come like he said he would. "Yeah, yeah, send him in, please. Thank you."

"Do you need anything?" Renee asked, as she stood to go. "Tea? Soup?"

"Maybe in a while. I'm okay for now."

Renee gently kissed his forehead, and then she and Brad walked out and Tobias walked in, messenger bag slung across the front of his dark coat, a worried look on his beautiful face. When had Aiden started thinking he was beautiful? *The minute you saw him*, his mind said. Yeah. Who was he kidding?

The witch closed the door behind him, then took in the room. The small dresser with a cloth on top, some coins, a ring, and a few books stacked on its surface.

"Chronicles of Narnia, huh?"

"Yeah. I love C.S. Lewis," Aiden said.

"Oh and Madeleine L'Engle! I *loved A Wrinkle In Time*."

"I still do," Aiden said, feeling the ghost of a smile tilting up his lips. "Sorry I can't sit up... I..."

"No, no, please."

Aiden motioned to the chair under the window. "Have a seat," he said.

Tobias pulled the chair closer, unslung the messenger bag and set it on the floor. It rustled and clinked. Then he took his coat off and flung it across the back of the chair. Aiden watched all of this as if it was the most interesting thing he'd ever seen. As though he could watch Tobias take his coat off forever.

He wore a burgundy sweater. It looked soft. The goatee that framed his mouth needed a trim. His eyes looked a bit drawn. His mouth was tight.

Aiden wanted to kiss the tightness away.

Finally, Tobias sat down and leaned over, peering at Aiden as though he could figure out what was wrong with him just by looking. Maybe he could.

"You don't look so good," Tobias said. "But actually, you look a lot better than I feared."

"Well, I don't know if I should say thanks." Aiden spoke softly. It felt as if speaking at normal volume was impossible.

"This is going to sound weird, but I was expecting your aura to be all cracked and shattered. But it's not. It actually looks strong. Your aura looks vibrant...and something's different about you."

"You mean besides this cracked skull I got?"

"No, it's not that. It's the fire in your heart," he said. "I can *feel* it now; it's growing stronger."

"How do you know about that?" Aiden whispered. He felt as if he could barely take a breath. "You're freaking me out."

Tobias reached out and tucked a lock of hair behind Aiden's ear. His touch was so gentle, like a warm whisper.

"I'm a witch, remember? I see things," Tobias said. "I see *you*."

Aiden just lay there quietly breathing for a moment. He wasn't sure what to say in response. Tobias turned away and began to rummage in the messenger bag on the floor.

"I made you some herbal formulas," he said. He pulled out two small dark brown bottles with stoppers in the top.

"What are they?" Aiden said.

"This one a combination of skull cap and St. John's Wort and a couple of other things that should be good for your head and concussion if you have one. It'll help with blood flow and help your healing process. And then this one"—he shook the second bottle—"is arnica, which is an herb traditionally used for bruising. I figured you must be bruised up."

"Yeah, I feel like my whole back must be black and blue. I'm kind of afraid to look at it."

"Well, just take this. Two droppers' full, two to three times a day."

"For how long?"

"As long as you need it. You'll know when to stop." Tobias smiled at him. "And I can always make more."

Tobias set the bottles on the bedside table and looked around the room again. His eyes wandered back to the dresser with the books on top.

"You kept the Brigid's cross."

"Yeah, thanks. It's nice. I never had one before."

"I made it."

"Yeah, you said that."

"Right. But I think I didn't realize," Tobias said, "that when I made it, I must have made it for you."

There was no thought in response. No words. Just a sudden wash of emotion so strong, Aiden couldn't even name it.

"I don't know what to say," Aiden said. "I don't even know how to feel." Some tears leaked out of his eyes. He wasn't sure if it was from the pain or the emotions. Tobias grabbed a tissue for him, and Aiden wiped his nose.

"I really like you, Tobias, but…"

"But I'm a witch."

"Yeah. But you're a witch. And I'm a Catholic. And I'm a little scared. And weird stuff is happening, and the cops are horrible, and Mary Jo's dead. And I'm *angry.* So angry. I just I'm not sure what to do. I'm…I'm kind of confused. Can you understand that?"

"I think so."

"Do you think you can be my friend?"

Tobias looked at him again and closed his eyes, drawing in a deep breath.

"Aiden, I want to be more than your friend, but I also think you're pretty awesome." He opened his eyes again. "And if being your friend is what I need to do, I'll do it. I just want to help heal you. That's what I want right now."

Aiden's eyes searched Tobias's face. "You know what I want?"

"What?" Tobias answered.

"I want you to help heal the people I work with. I want you to help heal this city. I want you to do a lot of things. Healing *me* doesn't mean that much; it's not enough."

A look of hurt flashed across that beautiful face.

"It's enough for me," Tobias said.

"It's not enough for me."

They sat quietly for a moment.

"Here, take some of this," Tobias reached for the bottles and drew some of the tincture into the stopper, then squirted first one round of herbs, and a second into Aiden's mouth.

Aiden winced, it was slightly bitter, slightly sweet. He swallowed it down.

"Thank you. Can you make a tincture for every house-less person in Portland?" he asked.

"I don't know," Tobias said, "maybe. Can I get you anything else?"

"Yeah," Aiden replied, "You can give me a kiss."

"Friends' kiss?"

"Friends' kiss."

"I'll take friendship then, while you figure out whether or not you want something more."

Tobias leaned forward again, smelling of fire, and incense, and warmth, and he placed the softest kiss on Aiden's lips. It was the polar opposite of the kisses they'd shared in the bar, and in Tobias's bed. Those had been hungry kisses, kisses that could bruise if they went on long enough.

But not this one. This one felt like chocolate melting on his lips.

Aiden hadn't known a kiss could feel that soft.

17

TOBIAS

The rain was growing colder. Tobias didn't care. He needed to be out here, outside in the garden behind his office. He breathed in the scent of pine and snuck his hand out of one of his gloves, tucking the glove into a coat pocket. He placed that hand, his left hand, the hand that was more sensitive and receptive, on the rough pine bark. Then he exhaled slowly, and breathed in again.

He needed a sign. A vision. A direction. His conversation with Aiden sat uncomfortably in his belly. A goad. A thorn. And clearly connected with the charge Brigid had laid upon him.

What did it mean to make a formula for a city? What did it mean to forge justice from the fires of love?

What did it mean to continue to create his life, a life that mattered?

Sheltered by the towering tree and its spreading, needle-covered branches, he was only half protected from the rain. It still dripped down his forehead, touching his nose and his lips. His wool hat soaked up the moisture. He tried to tune in to the tree, to the sense of it, the scent of it, the taste of it.

Sticking out his tongue, he waited to taste the rain itself. The droplets tasted slightly of the pine needles they fell from. The rain tasted of...a distant ocean. Sky. It also tasted of a slight foreboding. As if it was a harbinger of things to come.

Tobias returned his attention to the tree itself.

The tree was old, and deep, deep inside it, the sap ran slow, cold. He could barely feel it moving. But that didn't mean it wasn't there. He leaned his forehead against the tree, appreciating the welcoming solidity of it. Dropping his attention more deeply into his center, he simultaneously tuned into the energy field around his body, feeling where it merged with the pine.

This tree had sheltered squirrels and boring beetles, crows and woodpeckers, flickers, jays, ants, and worms for years and years. Far longer than Tobias been here. Far longer than Tobias had been alive.

He wondered what it must feel like, to be so old, and to have done your work so well. To have seen buildings built, children play, people weep, and laugh, and die. He wanted a life like that.

Lifting his head, he gazed up at the branches. The rain plopped from the needles and onto his cheeks.

Seeing Aiden had been a shock. He looked so pale, terrible, and half broken. Yet he was lit up inside with a fire Tobias couldn't help but respond to. The fire felt all-consuming, and Tobias wondered if there was any room in a man like that for anything outside his holy charge. He wondered if there was room for a man like him.

He wondered about that fire. It had Her fingerprints all over it.

"Brigid, what are you doing? Is there more to this plan I should know about? Some things I need to know?"

He hadn't thought much about justice in the past, but it was clear he needed to pay attention to it now. He'd been too focused on surviving with some part of him intact, and then on breaking away. Seeking his own freedom.

Helping others heal themselves was part of that freedom. But he knew that people like Moss and Aiden, more radical than he was, would likely say that without justice, freedom was a sham.

A breeze rustled the branches, sending more water raining down on his head.

Tobias hoped Aiden used the formulas. On his walk home, Tobias realized he'd taken to heart what Aiden had said about medicine for the city, and about helping the people that Aiden tried so hard to help every day. Tobias thought of his own tears, his sense of anger and helplessness, and realized how much of those emotions had been rooted in his fear.

He knew he needed to get inside, out of the rain, out of the coming ice that he could feel creeping up around the edges of his skin. The wind was really picking up now, whistling through the trees, causing a chill to rise on the back of his neck. He began to shake with the cold. But he couldn't leave this tree, not yet.

"You have something to tell me. I know it," he said. He took a breath and sank deeper.

:Go inside,: he heard.

"Inside the building?"

:Self:

Tobias tried to drop deeper, deeper still. He exhaled as slowly as he could, pausing before inhaling again, trying to match his heartbeat with the flow of the sap in the tree. So slow. Taking a long breath in of the icy air, he felt his eyes roll back in his head, seeking the other planes of existence. The places so often just beyond reach.

:Medicine,: the tree said.

"Yes. Yes," Tobias said, "you are medicine. You are good for congestion and coughs and helping people get the sickness out, remove it from their bodies."

:More,: he heard. *:Everything.:*

"Thank you," Tobias said. That was part of the answer.

He kissed the bark, feeling it rough under his mouth, then ran through the garden as white hail shattered the sky and bounced off the earth around his feet. He turned just as he hit the door, and watched the balls of ice bounce for a moment.

Then he went inside and ran up to his office, removing his coat as he went. Taking his hat off, he flung them both on a coat tree and entered his office space, wiping the moisture off his face.

He looked at the jars of herbs. There was a jar full of dried elderberries he had harvested in late summer. A jar of dried ginkgo leaves from just a few months before. They whispered to him now, the way the pine had.

Opening the wooden cabinet, he looked at the large jars of tincture he'd made up and stored. Some of them were still in process, others were ready now. What would he need? His eyes scanned the handwritten labels. Licorice, goldenseal, echinacea. He had them all. And there, on the bottom shelf in a jar full of brandy, were the inner layers of bark from the pine. He'd forgotten about it. It should be just about ready for use by now.

Thank you, he thought again, holding the image of the tree in his mind. *Thank you.*

He could do this. He knew it. *Don't forget what she said,*

Tobias, he said to himself. "Forge justice from the fires of love."

Once all the herbal tinctures and bottles were arrayed on his long work table, he took another breath and wiped more of the moisture from his face. Then he turned to his altar and lit a candle.

"Holy Brigid," he said, "show me. Tell me what I need to know. Help me make medicine to heal this city. Help me make a formula to ease the pain."

And then he turned, rolled up his sleeves, and prepared to put together as many formulas as he could from the tinctures he had on hand. He was suddenly filled with the urge to help as many homeless people in Portland as he could.

It wasn't just coming from Aiden. Part of it was the pledge to Brigid, he was certain of it. Part of it, though? Came from the conversation with his fucking father. His anger had honed the blade of his will. He was ready to *do* something now. To take his work to the next level.

He prayed it would be enough for now.

Make me into whatever weapon or tool you need, Brigid. I'm right here.

And as for a medicine for the city, he didn't know what that looked like yet. But he was damn well certain going to listen to these plants and tinctures and find out.

18

AIDEN

Long underwear, thermal shirt, flannel shirt, sweater, hoodie, wool hat, jeans, wool socks, boots. Big coat with the hood up.

It was still cold. Aiden was *freezing*. His nose felt as if it were about to fall off. The back of his skull ached, and was starting to pulse in time with his heartbeat. His back was on fire, his knees were on fire, his hips hurt.

Everything hurt and Aiden didn't care. He embraced the pain. *Jesus suffered, didn't he?* Aiden knelt on the sidewalk in front of the police station, determined and steadfast. Immovable.

The rain pelted him, the ice pelted him. There was nobody on the street today, except the occasional cop that ran past him, heading from the big glass doors on their way to a patrol car.

Aiden knelt, arms outstretched in the shape of a cross, heavy with the pain. His shoulders screamed. His biceps burned. His back was ready to seize up from the cold, the kneeling position, and yesterday's injuries.

And he was filled still with the holy fire.

Stingray had yelled at him before he went out, "You need to stay in bed. Are you crazy?"

"Yes," he had replied. "Yes, I am crazy."

Crazy with the certainty that he had to do this thing, no matter how little sense it made. He was under a compulsion and had to obey.

Aiden had slammed through the house, well, hobbled was more like it. But he had slammed drawers shut, slammed cupboards open, and forced himself to choke down some soup before he got dressed.

"I can't believe you're even up," Stingray had said. She'd followed him from his room to the kitchen to the living room, back to his bedroom again. She followed him until he finally thumped down the stairs and out the door.

"Aiden," she finally said, "please don't do this. Don't make me have to kill you."

"Well, if you do, that means *this* isn't going to kill me, doesn't it?" He had turned, clutching the cardboard under his arms, and looked back at his friend, his comrade, and said, "I'm sorry Stingray, but I have to go. I don't know what else to do and I have to do *something*. I can't just lie in bed all day."

"Well, then come with me to the kitchen. It's your shift day. I can put you to work." She was really pleading with him.

"I can't do that either," he said, then turned and walked toward the bus that would take him downtown. He really couldn't go to the soup kitchen; he was in no condition to lift anything. He supposed he could sit at a stool and chop vegetables or serve soup, but he couldn't bear the chatter. He couldn't bear the questions. He couldn't bear the concern.

So here he was, foolhardy, stupid, angry at himself,

angry for being in pain, angry at his body for betraying him. Angry at the cops, angry even at Mary Jo for freezing to death, which wasn't right.

He was so angry. Infuriated.

The rain and ice pounding him felt almost good, as they battered his already tortured body. It was as though he felt like he deserved the punishment of it. He needed to be punished for being so ineffective. And that made him angry too. That was old childhood perfectionist Catholic bullshit. He didn't even believe it anymore, except part of him clearly did. He was angry at Tobias for being a witch. Angry at himself for the fact that he was probably falling in love with that witch. And through it all, his heart still burned with whatever fire had him in its grips.

"St. Brigid, what do you want from me?" he cried out to the rain and the gathering dark. Though it was only midday, streetlamps were already lit, reflecting puddles that shone through the flying ice and rain. His body started to shudder and shake from the cold of it. He knew he wouldn't last much longer but he had to be here. He had to stay here for a little while.

A cop came over. "Hey buddy, you really need to get out of this."

Aiden looked at him, tight-lipped. "I'm praying," he said.

"Can't you pray somewhere else?"

"I'm praying for your soul," Aiden replied.

The cop just shook his head and walked away. *Praying for your soul.* The arrogance of it. But Aiden didn't care.

"Brigid," he said again, "what do you want from me?"

And then he heard a crash. The sound of a hammer beating steel. It repeated over and over in time with the beating of his heart and the pounding in his skull. And in the light of the streetlamp, he saw her.

She wore a long green mantle, and held burning flames in one hand, coiling up to lick at the rain, a woven cross in the other. She moved toward him. The flames and cross winked out of view. Her milk-white hands unhooked the clasp at her throat and she swung the mantle from around her shoulders. She wrapped the cloak around his back. Aiden was surrounded by a sense of warmth and love, peace and well-being. He could taste the sweetness of honey on his tongue and smell the scent of grass, as though he were kneeling, not on a city sidewalk, but in a vast field.

And then she touched his forehead and the pain in his head went away.

:*You are my child.*: Her voice was warm inside his head. :*Follow the path of love. Follow the fire in your heart.*:

She reached toward his chest with her flaming hand, igniting everything inside him. The pain rushed back in, worse than it was before. His body bucked and trembled. Ice and rain hissed as they met his coat and hat. Steam rose all around him. His eyes open wide, he stared into her two brown irises. Her eyes were huge. Her lips moved, forming words and sounds he could not understand. His skin felt as though it was being flayed from his muscles. His eyes rolled back in his head.

Over and over and over, her hands touched forehead, then chest. She whispered strange words into his left ear, then his right. The top of his head cracked open and flames rushed upward to the dark, wet sky.

And then she was gone. Aiden was left, arms upraised, body shaking, pelted once again by ice and rain.

No fire pouring from his head, though the top of his head tingled with warmth. No saint standing in front of him.

He began to cry. His eyes filled up. His nose filled up. It

took everything he had to not collapse forward onto the wet concrete sidewalk.

Aiden didn't know what she meant. He still didn't know what she wanted. But the aching in his head was finally gone. His back felt slightly better too. She had muted his pain. The fire had cleansed him.

He looked down and there was a green wool cloak, still wrapped around his shoulders, puddling on the sidewalk.

No.

"How is that possible?" he whispered. He lowered his arms, and touched the fabric. The wool was soft, with a slightly rough nap to it, beneath the fingertips that peeked out of his fingerless gloves.

"This is real," he murmured in wonder. "This is all real."

He closed his eyes for a moment, reveling in the warmth of the cloak protecting him from the rain. The trembling in his body slowed, and finally stilled.

He opened his eyes again, and the cloak was gone.

There was just gray concrete. Gray sky. Cold ice and rain.

19

TOBIAS

Tobias paused, and looked in through the open wooden gate at a courtyard filled with half barrel containers holding trimmed-back rose bushes, pink flowering winter camellias, and herbs. He could smell rosemary and sage, their scents released by the rain striking leaves.

The soup kitchen. *Aiden's* soup kitchen.

It was pouring rain. There were people huddled under a long overhang, eating soup, drinking tea, reading books, or talking. Dogs crouched under tables with bowls of water and kibble.

He shivered. "Good a time as any," he said, and walked through.

He nodded at some of the men. He looked around. Didn't see Aiden anywhere. Good. That meant he was still home in bed. Tobias admitted to himself that he wanted to make this first visit not under Aiden's watchful blue eyes. He wasn't exactly sure why he was nervous. Aiden was so clearly a man of purpose, and Tobias? He had a purpose as a healer, but this zeal for justice? It was new. He wanted to keep it to himself for a while, until he felt more comfortable with it all.

Pledges made to the Gods unfolded in their own time. And some of them needed to be held in the cauldron of silence.

Walking past the flowers, toward the sheltered overhang and the tables beneath it, he looked for someone who looked like they were in charge. Someone in an apron laughed with a few seated people at a corner table. Tobias didn't want to disturb the conversation.

There were two rust-painted steel doors ahead, with bright lights shining from the window to the left, so he opened one and entered a large brick dining room with big skylights, plants up in the rafters, and a long counter. People served soup, bread, and salad. Other workers bustled around behind them, and throughout the dining room. A few people lined up for the soup.

The air hummed with conversation and the clatter and clash of dishes moving from the wash sink to the rinse sink to some third sink that he wasn't sure what was for—sterilizing, maybe?

And against the back brick wall, a big altar filled with all sorts of statues and objects and religious items. It seemed like every religion was represented. He didn't see a pentacle. He grinned. Well, maybe someday he'd rectify that situation, but today was not that day.

"May I help you?" A short Black woman, wearing a red apron and a blue shirt, approached. She had dark hair, a brown, wide face, and friendly eyes. She was wiping her hands on a rag.

"I'm Tobias. Are you Stingray?"

She nodded, "You called. You're Aiden's friend."

He tried to stifle a blush at that. "Yeah. I met Aiden a

little while ago and he said that you might be willing to let me come in?"

She nodded. "You bring your herbs?"

"Yes, I've got them in my bag." He patted his messenger bag; the tiny bottles clinked inside.

"Well, let's get you set up. Do you need anything special?"

"Just a table and a chair."

"Okay. Grab a chair from that stack and I'll go get a folding table."

He turned around, and sure enough there was a stack of formed plastic chairs with metal legs against the brick wall near the metal doors. He grabbed one and looked around again. He wasn't sure where she wanted it.

He thought she had gestured over to the empty corner near the altar, and that seemed like as good a place as any to set up. He carried the chair over and had just set it down when Stingray came out from behind a closed door wrestling with a long folding table. He set the chair down and ran over to help.

"Thanks," she said. They snapped the legs out and set it up at an angle to the corner. "Just let me know when you're ready to start. I'll make an announcement."

"Thanks."

He saw people looking at him curiously. The rain pounded down on the skylight overhead and the smells of soup and bread and tea filled the air. It was a lot nicer here than he expected. Actually kind of warm and homey. He could see why Aiden loved it.

He set out several larger bottles, and a whole array of tiny, empty ones. He had filled some of the small bottles in advance, but he figured he'd ask people what they wanted or needed before filling the rest with the pre-made formulas. He raised a hand to let Stingray know she was ready, and she made the announcement. A moment later, an aproned volunteer came over and set a cup of tea down with a smile.

"Thank you," he said, and then the people started to approach. Some ragged, some clean, some who clearly looked like they had homes and jobs to go to and some who clearly lived on the streets. He hadn't expected that variety either. He expected everyone to be homeless—or houseless, as Aiden called them.

"I've got this cough," an Hispanic man said. "You got anything for that?"

"I do, pine bark. It's great for congestion and coughs. I'll give you some in a bottle," he said, filling one of the small vessels. "And then I have this, it's called Fire Cider and it's good for general health and immunity. So take the pine bark before your coffee for the next few days. But take the Fire Cider every day for as long as you can."

The Fire Cider was a staple, and he always made up plenty in advance of winter, so the ingredients had time to meld.

"How much?" the man said.

"Just one dropper full of each, every day."

"Thanks man."

And so it went for the next hour. People approaching, people thanking him. Some people wanted to stay and tell him their stories. That broke his heart. They seemed lonely, hurting. Some had a long list of grievances, others were just thankful someone was there to help.

Even the people with jobs and homes wanted help. He asked one woman about it. "If I don't eat here at least half the time, my money runs out by the end of the month."

What a way to live, he thought.

About an hour and a half later, the door crashed open

and there he was: Aiden, dark hair plastered to his face, drenched and shivering. Tobias had to force himself to stay in his seat and not rush forward. Aiden didn't even look at Tobias's corner; he just headed for the kitchen and disappeared behind the counter.

Tobias felt torn. There were a few more people waiting for help, and he didn't want to rush them, but he also knew that Aiden really didn't look so good. What was he even doing out of bed?

Finally the line died down. Tobias waited another ten or fifteen minutes, sipping at his tea, trying to stay calm and not think of Aiden as he watched the workers buzzing behind the counter or wiping up tables, bussing dishes, and cleaning up messes. It looked as though most of the guests were pretty good about bussing themselves, but there were a few—always, like anybody he guessed—who couldn't or didn't want to manage.

Finally, he couldn't stand it anymore. He packed up his bottles carefully, putting them back into his bag, and headed towards the counter. One of the dishwashers, a big burly white guy with his blond hair in a net and an industrial apron on, paused and said, "May I help you?"

"Yeah, I'm looking for Aiden. I saw him come back and I'm wondering if I could go through and say hello?"

"Sure man, head on back. He's probably in the break room."

Tobias squeezed between the dishwashers and another counter, past some long coffin freezers, and through another door into the back. Through there he faced a cement warren, with a washing machine and a dryer to the right, cubbies of what looked like donated clothes, and to the left, big racks filled with sacks of beans, rice, and onions. He could smell the papery onion smell and the yeasty, walnut-y scent of loaf after loaf of bread.

There was another door towards the back, so he moved towards it, hoping it was the break room. Sure enough, there was Aiden sitting in a chair, and Stingray bending over him. Aiden was toweling his head off and wiping his face. Stingray murmured something in a concerned tone.

Tobias knocked on the frame. "Sorry. I didn't mean to interrupt. I just wanted to say hello before I left."

"Tobias." Aiden looked startled. "I didn't know you were coming in!"

Tobias shrugged. "I didn't really either. But what you said... Well, I called in and Stingray said I could come. But I'm surprised you're even here, man."

Stingray snorted. "I'm surprised too. Someone was told to stay home and in bed. Someone instead went back out to kneel on the sidewalk *in front of the police station* in the pouring ice and rain. And someone is going to be sick and in the hospital very soon."

"Ease up, Stingray," Aiden said. "Please. I told you why I had to go out there."

"And I told you why you shouldn't. *You* talk to him," she said to Tobias, and shoved her way past him, out of the room.

Tobias entered, tentatively taking in the coffeepot, the day-old muffins and donuts, the chairs, a little bookcase, and a row of battered lockers. The room had definitely seen better days. The dining room was much nicer.

"Can I sit down?"

Aiden nodded.

"It's good to see you, but you really don't look so great."

"I know." Aiden paused. "What are you doing here?"

"You told me to help heal the people, heal the poor. So I

made up a bunch of formulas that I thought would work and here I am."

Aiden's face split into a wide grin at that. "Really? You brought a little clinic here?"

Tobias felt pleased, felt warmed inside. "Yeah, yeah I did."

"How'd it go? You gonna come back?"

"I think so. I liked it and the people seemed grateful."

Aiden nodded. "Most of the people here, they're always grateful. I'm grateful to come here every day."

"But you shouldn't have come today."

"No, I shouldn't. Stingray's so mad at me." He stared at Tobias for a moment, blue eyes looking feverish. "I'm not sure why I came by. I just needed a touchstone. I needed to remember..."

His voice wandered off, and he gazed at a corner of the room. Tobias wondered what he was seeing.

"You need to remember why you do this?" Tobias asked.

"Yeah. Can I tell you something weird?"

Tobias sat down and pulled a chair closer till their knees were almost touching.

"Tell me what?"

"She appeared to me again when I was kneeling in the rain."

"Who?"

"St. Brigid."

Oh boy. She was everywhere. If Tobias ever had any question that the Goddess had a plan, that question was gone now.

She clearly did.

"Let's get you out of here," he said.

20

AIDEN

Tobias took Aiden home with him.

They clattered up the front steps to yet another Portland Craftsman. Aiden tried to keep from shivering, standing on the broad porch as Tobias got out his keys and got the heavy front door open.

"Hey Reece, Freddie, this is Aiden. Aiden, my housemates." Tobias's voice sounded clipped and annoyed. Aiden wondered what was up.

Reece and Freddie—Aiden realized he had no idea which was which—were a man and a woman sitting on a green couch, hanging out in the book-lined living room, drinking beer and playing some sort of geeky card game on the coffee table. They seemed nice enough, but Aiden barely even registered they were there. Luckily, Tobias steered him upstairs to his room right away.

Once they got settled in, Aiden realized he really wasn't coping very well. This was all too new. Too raw.

Tobias's bedroom was a magical place. It smelled like him. Like frankincense, myrrh, with undertones of burning wood, and the sweetness of a man. There were prints of plants and flowers on the green walls, and there was the high, wooden bed. Aiden felt his face flush with the memory of it. He almost wished he wasn't so messed up and exhausted.

But he also hoped Tobias didn't push him. Not tonight. Not when everything felt like too much. His body was doing better after whatever St. Brigid had done, but it still felt pretty battered. And emotionally? He wasn't ready for sex again. Not just yet.

Tobias helped Aiden off with his clothes, so gently. Almost lovingly. Once he was undressed down to boxer shorts and a T-shirt, Tobias handed him a pair of gray sweatpants, pulled back the forest green comforter, revealing burgundy striped sheets, and tucked him into that high bed.

"I'm going to run your clothes down to the dryer, okay? Be right back."

Aiden lay on that high bed, feeling warm and snug for the first time all day. He closed his eyes, and relaxed against the pillow. Images of the saint flickered behind his eyelids. She felt like an ally. A protector. And she had healed him, which felt like a miracle he didn't deserve.

When Tobias came back, he shut the door behind him and then undressed. Aiden watched as he unveiled his white limbs, shucking off jeans and layers of sweater and a flannel shirt, until there he stood in boxer briefs and a T-shirt. Aiden couldn't take his eyes off of him. His fingers clutching the edges of the comforter as though it was a life raft and he was at sea. Tobias pulled on a pair of navy sweats, padded to the bed, and smiled down at Aiden before crawling in and propping himself up, leaning against the headboard on a couple of pillows.

Without a word, he held out his arms. Aiden crawled up, and Tobias tucked him into the crook between his shoulder and his chest. Aiden could feel his soft breath ruffling the edges of his hair.

Finally the rage, the confusion, and the humming vibration that had been with Aiden for days uncoiled itself.

"Do you want to talk about it?" Tobias asked.

Aiden lay there for a moment, just breathing. Just enjoying the scent of Tobias and the feel of his arm around his shoulder. Enjoying the feeling of his thigh tucked over Tobias's legs. Aiden rested his right hand, palm down, on Tobias's chest. The T-shirt was soft, as though it had been washed a hundred times.

"I'm not even sure how to talk about it. All I know is...I was kneeling, praying, and the rain and the hail were beating down on me. I could tell my body was reacting to that, but inside I felt like I was on fire. And then Brigid was just there. Like, I actually *saw* her."

Tobias scooted a little further down in the bed, still facing up. Aiden adjusted his body to match, sinking more deeply under the comforter the blankets, the soft sheets.

"What did she look like?" Tobias asked. His voice was soft, soft like the candlelight in the room, soft and warm like the scent of beeswax. "Did she say anything?"

The saint was so clear in Aidan's mind, that vision of her and her green mantle, standing in the pouring ice and rain. He didn't think he would ever forget that sight. But he also had no idea how to explain it. Because he didn't understand it himself.

Aidan took a breath and tried again. "She had this green cloak on. It fell from her shoulders to the sidewalk. In my head, for some reason I called it a mantle. I don't know why. She had fire in one hand, and that woven cross in the other. She put her mantle around me. She wrapped me in the cloak."

Aiden could feel Tobias take a huge breath. He released it with a mighty sigh. "Do you know how lucky you are? I don't know anyone else who's had a vision like that, just out on the street with a Goddess walking toward them. Did it feel like that mantle was real?"

"It *was* real. I saw it puddling around me on the sidewalk and I could feel it, too. And then I closed my eyes for a minute. When I opened them again, it was gone."

Aiden leaned back and looked up into Tobias's brown eyes. "I feel calm. Like everything's going to be all right. Like she's with me now, but..."

Tobias ran a hand down Aidan's cheek and cupped his chin from before dropping his hand. "But what?"

"But I'm also scared. I mean, who has visions like that?"

Tobias gave a little laugh. "Apparently gay Catholics who are crazy enough to pray on the sidewalk in a hailstorm."

Aiden had to smile. He leaned in and kissed Tobias, and settled his head back on the man's shoulder. "All I've been doing is talking about myself," Aiden said. "What's been happening with you?"

Tobias squeezed Aiden's shoulder. Aiden nestled himself closer.

"Nothing as exciting as you. I spent my morning talking to a pine tree." He laughed again; Aiden felt the rumble of it in his chest. "And then Brigid told me to get my ass back to work. She does that sometimes. And I made a bunch of formulas from some tinctures I had on hand, called up the soup kitchen, and here we are."

"Can I ask a question?"

"Sure."

"What's magic?"

Aidan felt Tobias scooch up again and pull away a little

bit. He felt a flush of panic for a moment, as though he done something wrong.

"I'm sorry, is that not okay to ask?"

"Of course you can ask. I just was thinking I could use a cup of tea or a glass of wine if we're going to have this kind of conversation. You feeling better?"

Aiden realized he *did* feel better. He felt safe here. Cared for. So he nodded. "Yeah, I am, and you know what? I think I would like a glass of wine."

Tobias kissed his forehead, slid out of the bed, and said, "I'll be right back. And I want to tell you a story about magic, and Brigid's mantle. It's pretty cool and I think you'll like it."

Aiden eased back onto the pillows, looked up at the pale blue ceiling of Tobias's room. The muscles of his stomach and his shoulders felt relaxed for the first time in days. He never had this before, never had a person he could lie in bed with and talk about important things.

"God, I'm not sure why you brought me a witch, but I guess I'm supposed to learn something from this. And whatever your reasons are, I want to thank you."

His eyes had rested on the bedroom altar with its candles, the long double-sided blade, the polished stick of wood. And a statue of Brigid, with a woven cross leaning against it.

"And thank you, Brigid. I'm still not sure where this is leading, but I'm willing to find out."

The flame inside his chest flickered.

Aiden had a feeling the journey was going to be interesting, at least.

21

TOBIAS

The light coming in the window was shadowy and blue. It must be just before dawn.

Eyes closed, Tobias lay in bed, curled on his side, letting his brain slowly turn over, waking up a little more with every breath of the cold morning air. He felt it then, entering his awareness. It was a sense that something had changed. Not a cataclysmic shift. Nothing like what Aiden had described going through. But he felt different. More alive.

Letting his breathing deepen, he opened his awareness outward. And it was a whole new world out there. He felt plants talking outside his bedroom window, as leaves reached for the rain. He heard the pots of herbs in the kitchen. He could smell the trees, even through the double layers of glass.

And his skin felt alive, as though the experience of resting in soft cotton was brand new. His skin was so sensitive, he felt his nipples harden under his T-shirt. His fingertips softly stroked the sheet covering the bed.

The coffee brewing down the stairs smelled amazing.

His brain kicked in, and marveled at the talking plants,

and the deep sense he had of them. He usually only connected that clearly after a long meditation. Never had he awakened like this and felt and heard life going on around him like this. *I should make a grief formula for Sara's family,* he thought.

Tobias heard Aiden's soft breathing behind him. Still asleep. They had ended up spooned against each other last night, starting with Tobias on the outside, but clearly, they had rolled over at some point and reversed positions. That felt amazing, too. And as if Aiden being here was another piece in whatever this awakening was. That they'd both had a shitty day, and been drawn to that bar. That Brigid had a hand on both of their lives. That they both clearly needed healing. Different kinds of healing, and Tobias was only now admitting he needed that, but yeah, healing just the same.

The plants were everything to Tobias. Plants and coven. And now, if he dared hope for it, even the beginnings of love.

For the first time in a long while, Tobias remembered what a *gift* the plants were. The coven had studied the Norse runes a few years back, and the one letter that always stuck out for him was the gift rune, gebo. It looked like a big X. "The joining of two disparate forces," Raquel had said. "A joyful obligation."

Working with the herbs *was* a joyful partnership. Tobias had just gotten so wrapped up in his own emotional states that he'd forgotten.

But the plants and herbs never forgot. They were always there, ready to teach him, ready to offer their medicine, always ready to continue the cycles of death and life and rebirth.

He stretched, and felt Aiden's warmth curled up against

him. Another gift. Goddess, Tobias felt lucky right then. Aiden responded to his movement, snuggling closer, and placed a soft kiss on his T-shirt, right on top of his shoulder blade.

Tobias loved spooning, but right now, he wanted to hold Aiden more tightly.

He rolled over, and wrapped his arms and legs around Aiden's body, and kissed his forehead.

"This is the best thing in the world," he said.

"Mmmm. Good morning," Aiden murmured.

"How do you feel?"

Aiden exhaled with a soft, little sound, then rubbed a hand across his eyes.

"Pretty good. Still a little bruised, and emotionally exhausted, but I swear, that visitation from Brigid—even though it still freaks me out—helped me. I'm better. A lot better."

"I'm glad. Do you have to get to work?" Tobias placed kisses around Aiden's eyes, down his cheekbones, and at the edges of his mouth.

Aiden groaned. "I do. I'm probably already late. Got to stop making a habit of that."

"I'm a bad influence," Tobias said. "But I don't want you to leave. Not yet."

"Five more minutes," Aiden agreed, shifting his face sideways, until their lips met, so warm in the frigid morning air. The kisses were gorgeous. Tobias didn't want them to stop.

Finally, Aiden paused for a breath.

"Hey, Tobias?"

"Mmm?"

"I like being friends with you so far."

Tobias could feel the smile behind the words. It made

him feel...glad. And as though anything might be possible. As though the plants and the trees and the air and Aiden's lips were all part of a new life. A good life.

Fuck his parents. He'd figure out a way to make this work. He had to. And today? It seemed as though the universe agreed.

Tobias felt inside his bones that he would get the support he needed.

"I like being friends with you, too. But the plants are actually calling me today, which means it's a good day to get to work. And if I want you to keep spending the night here, I guess I've got to let you get to work, too. Besides, I don't want Stingray mad at me."

He flung back the layers of bedding, and the icy air hit his exposed skin. Aiden gasped.

"The only way out is through," Tobias said.

"I know, but does it have to be this cold? Doesn't your household believe in turning on the heat?"

Tobias shrugged slightly, scrambling out of sweatpants and into long underwear and jeans. A flannel shirt and a black sweater went over the T-shirt. Sorry as he was that they hadn't had sex in the night, he was also happy to not feel the need for a shower. He'd take one that night. Right now? He wanted to keep as much of his body covered as he could.

"We're pretty frugal and keep the thermostat set low at night. I can go bump it up in a minute, though if all we're doing is getting ready to leave, it seems silly."

He could see Aiden, moving a little more slowly than he was, looking around for his clothes. He looked a lot better today, which was good. Brigid really had done something to help, Tobias didn't doubt it now. There was no way Aiden should be moving this well after the battering he'd taken.

"Oh, shit!" Tobias said. "I put your clothes in the dryer last night! They were wet. Let me run and grab them. Get back in the bed!"

Tobias ran down the stairs and to the little porch just off the kitchen. He loaded the dry clothes into his arms, and raced back to his room.

Aiden was wrapped in the comforter, staring at the altar. Transfixed. His face looked as though he'd been talking with Gods or angels. It stopped Tobias dead. It felt as though he were in the presence of someone holy. Someone so beautiful, Tobias wasn't even sure how they could be real. He. Aiden. How Aiden could be real.

But he was. And he was in Tobias's bedroom, wrapped up in blankets from his bed.

Tobias cleared his throat. "I have your clothes." He shut the door. Aiden reached his arms out, and it took everything Tobias had to not walk straight into those outstretched arms. He handed Aiden the small pile of clothing instead.

"Thanks."

As Aiden got dressed, Tobias laced his boots on, and found a scarf and jacket.

"I saw you looking at the altar. Do you want to pray with me before we leave?" he asked, once Aiden was dressed.

Aiden turned those blue eyes on his, and nodded. "Yes. If that's okay with you."

Tobias began his simple morning ritual. He counted his breaths out loud, so Aiden could follow. Inhaling for four. Pausing for four. Exhaling for four. Pausing for four. They breathed until Tobias felt centered, which, given his state this morning, didn't take long.

Tobias struck a match, which hissed and sparked. The scent of sulfur scratched at his nose. The taper on the altar flared to life.

The men stood next to one another in silence for a moment, saying their own private prayers.

After five minutes, Tobias took a deep breath, and spoke out loud.

"Holy Brigid, we thank you for your presence in our lives. We ask for your blessing. We offer our service. If there is any information you feel we need to complete the tasks you have set us, or help to walk the road of our destinies, please speak it to us in sign, symbol, or word."

The air around the altar shimmered. The candle flame shot up four inches and began to waiver. The edges of his sight grew strange, as though someone were bending the light in the room, and the air felt thick. He was partially terrified, partially excited.

Aiden grabbed his hand.

Tobias squeezed Aiden's fingers back and didn't let go. He stared at the candle, then heard a strange, half-strangled noise come from Aiden's throat.

He turned, and saw Aiden's face change. It was flushed with heat, and his eyes fluttered behind closed lids, those long dark lashes touching his cheeks. His mouth grew slack, as though every muscle in his face had relaxed. As though he were somewhere else.

Tobias just waited next to him, holding his hand, sensing the energy, knowing something was happening, but not knowing exactly what.

He'd seen this state sometimes, with Brenda or Tempest or Raquel. Sometimes even Alejandro. When a deity was about to speak through him, his face looked that way, too.

But he never seen it outside of his coven. He was beginning to think Aiden was a true mystic.

Tobias finally broke the silence with a whisper. "What is she telling you?"

Aiden's mouth opened and shut a few times as though it were trying to form words but couldn't quite. Then he licked his lips, just a flicker of red tongue out and back again.

"She's telling us to prepare. Battle is coming. Battle is here."

The room grew even colder. Tobias could see Aiden's breath as it puffed out from his lips.

"Brigid? What other message do you have? How should we prepare?"

He waited, staring at this man he loved so dearly already. Nothing.

Finally, Aiden shook his head and opened his eyes.

"That's all she said," Aiden told him, eyes blinking.

Tobias turned back to the altar. The candle flame burned steadily again. A low, sedate flame.

"Brigid? What do I need to know?"

He dropped his attention to his center, then expanded it outward. There was the rain. There was a squirrel. There was the Japanese maple, nude of all its leaves. There was a stand of crocus. There was the rosemary bush.

And here was Aiden. And Tobias.

And her message to Tobias was as clear as the speech of the plants. As clear as if the Goddess had dropped the words directly into his brain.

Healing, and easing grief, and preparing for battle, were all of equal importance. He saw that. He *felt* it. He wasn't sure why he hadn't understood before.

22

AIDEN

"We need more salad!" Renee called out over the din of the kitchen and dining room. Lunch rush was in full swing; there was a line out the rust-colored metal doors, and the dining room was practically full.

It was all hands on deck at the soup kitchen. Aiden was still a little sore, and slightly shaky, but he had to admit Tobias's herbal formulas were helping. Hanging out with Tobias the night before had helped, too. He smiled as he rushed to the coffin freezers, where two volunteers chopped mounds of cabbage and lettuce, throwing the vegetables into a giant metal bowl. One of them added handfuls of shredded carrots, and the croutons that the morning breakfast crew had baked before they left.

A lot of people said they never ate croutons anywhere but De Porres House of Hospitality, that's how good they were: garlicky and crisp, made with fresh herbs grown by one of the cooks in his garden.

"Is this almost ready?" he asked.

The two volunteers, middle-aged women who must have

taken early retirement, looked up at him. He really should learn everyone's names, but had learned to wait until he knew they were coming back. Stingray was great at learning everyone's names the first day. That was probably why she was crew chief and Aiden wasn't.

"We just need to dress it, and then you can take it away," one of the women said.

He watched as one of the women poured the oil, vinegar, and herb mixture from a gallon jug into the bowl. The other woman held two giant serving spoons and mixed the cabbage, romaine lettuce, and croutons and carrots, blending the whole thing together until the salad was evenly dressed.

Aiden's stomach growled. He wasn't going to have time to eat lunch for a while.

Hoisting the big bowl in his arms, he winced. Lifting it was a mistake. It was straining the muscles in his back. He should've known better, but when they were in this kind of a hurry, it was just easier to do things himself. Besides, he thought he was in better shape than he apparently was. He was more healed than he had any right to be, but that didn't mean his body wasn't still paying the price of all the punishment it had taken.

He walked as quickly as he could across the red-tiled kitchen floor towards the salad station where a clean, upturned garbage can waited. That would be the pedestal for the salad bowl. He heaved it down.

"Thank you," Renee said. Then she spared him a glance. "You doing okay?" Aiden just shook his head and shrugged, which caused him to wince again.

"I'll be fine."

He rolled his shoulders, trying to ease the aching, and

looked around the kitchen. It looked like things were under control for the moment. That meant he should go and check the floor, see if everything was okay out in the yard.

He skirted the soup and salad line and hit the long bar on the metal doors, walking out into the outdoor dining area. Brad was washing one of the giant soup pots, which was propped up on a milk crate, using a hot water hose and a lot of soap.

"Hey man," Brad said. "Someone here to see you. I told her she had to wait. That we're slammed today."

"Who is it?"

"I don't know. Looks like some politician to me."

Aiden looked around and finally spotted a woman in a navy peacoat, neat navy slacks ending in quality brown leather boots. A brown plaid scarf wrapped around her neck. Her skin was about three shades darker than the scarf and her hair was perfectly groomed, with soft waves falling around her face. She was pretty. Subtle makeup, clearly firmly middle-class. And Brad was right, she had the look of politician about her. Aiden thought she even looked familiar.

He walked toward where she was standing, near one of the flowering pink camellia bushes. It wasn't raining, so it was nice to be out in the garden despite the cold.

She held out a hand encased in supple brown leather. "Aiden? Thanks for coming to speak with me."

Definitely a politician.

Aiden shook her hand. "I'm sorry, do I know you?"

"Is there anyplace we can talk?"

"This isn't good enough?"

She stammered a moment, practically sputtering. "I mean, it's really beautiful out here, but..."

"You'd like someplace more private."

She nodded, relief easing some of the lines of tension in her face. He let her off the hook, then shook his head to himself, not sure why he did that. Old, ingrained habits. Always put middle-class or rich people at ease. You think he would've learned better by now.

"Follow me."

He led her into the tiny, cement block office behind the kitchen pantry. It was in the opposite corner of the building from the break room, separated by the racks of beans and rice.

Two battered metal desks sat at right angles with a small aisle between them. They were covered with pens and calendars, and flanked by file cabinets stuffed with resources for people who lived on the streets, or needed mental health care, or a free dentist. A corkboard bristled with notices for rape crisis centers and places in the city to get showers. One small section of the board was reserved for guests they'd had to kick out, small pieces of paper relating what their offense was and how many days they were ousted for.

That was Aiden's least favorite part of the job, telling someone they'd broken enough community agreements that they had to stay away for thirty days.

He motioned to a battered rolling desk chair. "Have a seat."

He had to give the woman credit. She didn't bat an eyelash before she sat.

He sat in the other desk chair across from her and just watched her, waiting. She plucked the soft gloves off her fingers, smoothed the brown leather, folded the thumb back and set the gloves on her lap. He noticed she didn't unwind her scarf or unbutton her coat. She wasn't planning to stay long.

"I'm Terry Benson. From the city council."

So that was where he recognized her from. He had started attending city council meetings on occasion around a year ago when the community decided they needed to keep a finger on the pulse of city government.

"And? We're pretty busy today, so I'd appreciate it if you let me know why you wanted to talk with me."

Her lips were tight. Her deep brown eyes searched his face for a moment, as if trying to decide whether or not she could trust him.

She finally spoke again. "This needs to be on the down low. But I heard about your vigil in front of the police station. You've poked the hornets' nest, you know?"

Aidan shrugged. "I'm not out there in the rain and hail trying to make anyone feel comfortable."

She ignored that remark.

"How much do you remember about the building fires and the accusations against the developers last month?"

"Carter," he said.

She nodded.

Carter was a greedy, greedy man.

"All I know is he was yet another developer who didn't want to adhere to the low-income-housing rules and decided he was better off torching his job sites and collecting insurance money, right? And it seemed for a minute like the mayor had something to do with it, but I haven't heard anything further than that."

She leaned forward, the old chair creaking and groaning under her as she moved.

"The mayor is in it up to his neck." She said. "And the chief of police, too."

"And you're telling me all of this why?"

She looked around the office. He didn't know whether she was seeing the space at all or just making sure that no one was listening.

"Because I think it's all connected."

Aiden was growing impatient. "Look, Ms. Benson, I really don't have time for this. I have a lot of people to help feed. So could you cut to the chase, please?"

She sighed, and finally unwound the scarf from around her neck, then leaned back in her chair again. Terry Benson opened her mouth and then closed it again. She was clearly thinking. Aiden tapped his fingers on the arm of the chair. He could feel his anger coming back. He didn't know if that was good or not. Maybe that was part of preparing for battle.

A battle he was realizing had its first lines drawn for him when he refused those cops entry to the kitchen garden.

"I wanted you to know that it's all connected. The police sweeps of the camps, the raids, the fires, the mayor, the developers."

Aidan took in a sharp breath. Now it was his turn to lean forward. Hands on his knees, he stared her down. She stared right back.

"And what do you want me to do about it?"

She looked around again, then lowered her voice. "I want you to know, you and your friends, that if you want to take them down... A lot of us on the city council will support you."

Then she stood up so suddenly the chair squealed and rocked on its base. She wrapped that plaid scarf back around her neck, slid her fingers into those supple brown gloves, and looked up at him again.

"Them? Who exactly are 'them?'"

"I think you can figure it out. That's all I've got," she said. "I just needed to let you know."

Aiden closed his eyes for a moment, trying to take it in. This wasn't as weird as a saint coming up to him on a sidewalk, but it was plenty weird all the same.

"Message received. I'll walk you out the gate."

23

TOBIAS

After Aiden called from the soup kitchen with his bombshell, Tobias set aside his herbs and formulas and called the coven. They decided to meet at Raquel's house, since they had planned to have a coven meeting about the Interfaith Council and the work they needed to do anyway.

Only half the coven could show up early. The rest planned to join in later. They'd just have to get filled in.

Alejandro was here, and Cassiel. Raquel, of course, and Lucy.

Tobias and Cassiel were in the living room. Tobias sat on Raquel's overstuffed red couch, and Cassiel sat on one of the big chairs that were arranged in front of a crackling fireplace. Raquel had put some rosemary and lavender onto the burning logs. The herbs perfumed the air. Tobias approved.

"How's work?" Cassiel asked.

"It's...amazing, actually. Its funny, I had a huge fight with my father about it this week, and was feeling all bent out of shape. But since our ritual, and all the other stuff that's been happening, it feels like something has snapped into place."

Lucy and Alejandro were in the kitchen making tea and getting drinks for people. Tobias could hear Raquel talking to her son, Zion, who was also in the kitchen doing homework.

Tobias scratched his head. "My clients today were great. The herbs and formulas were practically singing. And people responded. They were telling me dreams and visions they were having. Good ones. And one of them told me I needed to start charging more. He left me a tip. No one ever leaves me a tip."

Cassiel had her feet tucked up under her thighs, head propped on one hand, cascade of orange curls falling down across her shoulders. She looked good. Her new relationship seemed to be agreeing with her, and she seemed to have made some peace with her ability to speak to ghosts.

Tobias was glad. He knew that had been quite a struggle. Everyone had to go through a fight with their gifts, it seemed. Just like he'd been fighting with his own. Hopefully the little breakthroughs he'd been having would continue, and it wouldn't be as painful as he'd feared.

Between the hammer and the anvil, Brigid. For as long as it takes, I'm yours.

"That's so great, Tobias. It sounds like it might be a sea change for you."

"I think you're right."

He looked over the fireplace, where a large painting of a Tarot card hung. The Sun. Joy. It was a portrait of Zion at a younger age, running with his arms out, and radiating rays of yellow and orange lighting up the sky. It represented life-giving warmth. And joy.

The doorbell rang. Tobias leapt up from the couch to get it. Opening the big wooden front door, he saw Aiden standing on the porch, and couldn't help but smile.

"Hey there," Tobias said.

"Hey there yourself," Aiden replied. His smile felt warmer than the fire in the hearth.

Tobias pulled him into the house, shutting the door behind him, and wrapped his arms around Aiden in a big hug, breathing in the cold clinging to his clothing and his skin. He squeezed his arms beneath the bulge of Aidan's backpack, just above where his hips met his lower back. Then he leaned away, smiling, waiting for permission for a kiss.

Aiden still had his own smile splitting his face. Tobias leaned an inch closer. Aiden did too. They crept forward, inch by inch, until by mutual agreement, their lips met in a soft welcome. The kiss deepened. Growing more insistent. Oh Goddess. Tobias could kiss this man all night.

"I'm sitting right here!" Cassiel called out from the living room.

The two men separated, laughing, and Tobias stepped backwards and waved him through the foyer towards the living room.

"Come on in. You can put your stuff anywhere. Only half of us could make it to this meeting, but we'll fill the rest of the coven in later tonight." Aiden slung his backpack off his shoulders set it next to the couch.

"Hi, I'm Aiden." He held out a hand to Cassiel. She reciprocated.

"Cassie. I saw you at the meeting the other night, but it's great to meet you officially."

Tobias swung the kitchen door open to alert the rest of the coven that their guest was here, then came back out and sat next to Aiden on the couch. Raquel, Alejandro, and Lucy all greeted him as they entered the room. Raquel handed him a mug of steaming mint tea.

"Welcome to my home," she said.

"Thanks. It's a beautiful place. How did you know I like mint tea?"

Raquel tapped her head. "Psychic," she said.

Tobias sipped his own tea, a combination of mint and fennel. It was delicious. Then he turned to Aiden and raised an eyebrow. "Do you want to tell them what you told me? Or should I?"

Aiden leaned forward and set his tea on the long, low coffee table in front of the sofa. Then he sat back.

"I know some of you heard me speak at the interfaith meeting, and I met a couple of you, I think, but I was a little overwhelmed that night." He gave a wry little smile at that. Tobias hoped he wasn't embarrassed. Aiden had been *brilliant* that night.

"I don't know how many of you know this, but myself and some of the other workers at the kitchen went out to try to help a houseless camp the last time the cops did a sweep." He rubbed the back of his skull. "I got cracked on the head pretty good that day."

"By a cop?" said Lucy.

"A cop pushed me," Aiden said. "And I fell backwards onto a rock. It knocked me out. I'm still a little sore from it. Tobias's herbs have been helping, though."

"And Brigid," Tobias murmured.

Aiden nodded, and took another sip of tea. "Since then, I've been praying in front of the police station to protest the sweeps. The cops have been threatening lately. Even before then, they were showing up at the kitchen, looking for people, and getting pissed off when we wouldn't let them in. But that's not why I'm here. I'm here because today, this city council member came to the soup kitchen to talk to me."

Raquel crossed her arms over her chest. There was an extra crease on her forehead. "And what was that about?"

"She wanted to tell me that the police sweeps, the construction site fires, the weird, hinky stuff with the mayor, and maybe even the chief of police, were all connected."

Cassiel jerked. Tobias looked over and saw that she looked more pale than was even her usual. She clutched the edges of her sweater together as though there was an inner chill she needed to stave off.

"I should have known it wasn't over," she said. "I should have known we didn't have much of a rest coming."

"What do you mean?" Aiden asked.

Cassiel looked at Tobias. Tobias lifted his hands and shrugged his shoulders. "It's your story more than anyone else's here," he replied.

Cassie took a big breath, and sipped at her own tea. Everyone just waited. She would speak when she was ready. She closed her eyes for a moment, as though she were praying. Or remembering. When she opened them, she trained them steadily at Aiden's face. Tobias could almost feel the weight of her gaze; she had that spookiness in her eyes she got sometimes, when some big magic was trying to come through. Like when she talked to ghosts.

"We are the ones who figured out the mayor was working with that developer, Carter. I don't know how much Tobias has told you about the coven, but we got the information because I was helping someone with a ghost. The ghost happened to be the dead reporter who'd been hot on a story and was killed for it."

Aiden sat his mug down again. He leaned slowly back on the couch and raked his fingers through his hair, keeping hands laced around his skull as if he was trying to keep the thoughts in. "You have to be kidding me."

Tobias wanted to touch him so badly, but Aiden needed to navigate this on his own. Aiden would either spook and run, or he'd figure out they were for real.

"She's not kidding, Aiden," Alejandro said. "And I think you wouldn't be here if you weren't having some strange experiences of your own. We've all had them. That's why we work together. Look at me." He gestured to his slender form. He was dressed in a neat, pale blue dress shirt under a purple cashmere pullover. Nice, black, knife-creased wool slacks met fancy black leather shoes on his feet. "If you need computer work done, I'm top in my field. I dress this way because people give a man in a dress shirt more money than they give a man in a T-shirt and jeans, but this clothing doesn't mean I'm not a brujo. And it doesn't mean I haven't seen some uncanny shit."

Aidan exhaled, pushing the air past his lips in a whoosh. "Okay. Okay, I can get that. At least I'm willing to for now."

Tobias cleared his throat. "So now that we have this information, I feel like it changes everything we talked about at the Interfaith Council. We have some vital information that the rest of those people *don't* have. So I'm wondering what we're going to do with it? We are having our meeting tonight anyway, and I propose we do some magic about this."

Tobias looked around the living room. The only sounds were the crackling of the fire, and Zion's distant humming as he did homework in the kitchen.

"I propose that, just like we did a working to take down that developer, Carter, we do some magic to figure out how to help these houseless people. That's the least we can do, right? But what I'd rather do is pull down the entire house of cards."

Aiden cleared his throat. Right. There was that, too.

Tobias sighed. "And there's one more piece of information that's not on the table yet. Brigid came to us this morning. She had another message."

He exchanged a glance with Aiden.

Aiden spoke. "She told us to prepare. That a battle was coming. That it was almost here."

Lucy stood up and started pacing in front of the big stone fireplace. She shook her hands, as if she was shaking out spirits or demons. She started speaking as she walked. "We need to catch the pattern. We need to see the web. We see all the flies"—she stopped and looked at everyone, —"but I think we haven't yet figured out who exactly the spider is."

Tobias found himself nodding. "I think you're right, Lucy. And I say we bring the battle to their door. Let's figure out how."

"Oh. And there's one more thing," Aiden said. "I didn't mention it before, Tobias, because so much has been going on, and because frankly, it feels like bullshit."

"What's that?"

"The Interfaith Council is meeting tonight. Without you."

"On purpose?"

Aiden just gave him a look.

"Fuck them," Lucy said. "They're going to need us before all of this is through."

"I'm heading there now to convince them of it," Aiden said.

Tobias crossed the room and kissed Aiden, right in front of the whole coven. Aiden kissed him back. Then Tobias helped him up and walked him to the door.

"If you want to come over after the meeting tonight, just text me, okay?"

"Okay."

Tobias folded Aiden into his arms, and breathed him in for a moment. "Stay safe for me, will you?"

They kissed again, long and slow this time. Then Aiden went off into the cold and dark.

Tobias had asked Aiden to stay safe, but Tobias? He all of a sudden knew that *he* wasn't safe at all. He had fallen, hard and fast, for that man. And plants and trees were talking to him in the rain. And Brigid was preparing him for battle.

Tobias realized he was glad. Fiercely glad. Life was dangerous. And it was all a gift.

24

AIDEN

J aqueline was having trouble keeping control of the meeting, though Lord knew she was trying.

What amazed Aiden was that he *knew* she was a very skilled facilitator—it was why she always got picked to lead meetings. But nothing was helping that night. The warring camps in the meeting room were having none of it. They would not be placated on either side. Aiden couldn't blame them. His own fury was back, except the anger he had felt for the police was now directed at the people in this room.

They were back in the meeting room and diminished in numbers, because after someone had decided to exclude the coven, some of the Buddhists had quit in disgust. Aiden hoped they'd be back. He felt badly even being here. He hadn't expected to meet with the coven tonight, and felt guilty about not mentioning it to them before.

He had little patience with petty interfaith infighting, and with everything else going on, it had felt stupid to drag the coven into it. He felt better having at least mentioned it, he had to admit. Like he wasn't keeping a secret anymore.

If it turned out the coven needed to do this work on their own, that might even be a good thing. At least they wouldn't have to put up with this bullshit.

Reverend Laney was in full voice tonight, which, considering that his voice was scratchy and harsh, wasn't a pleasant experience. An older white gentleman, vest straining slightly over a small pot belly, he was on his feet and shouting at Rabbi Schwartz in front of the whiteboard. The rabbi leapt up from her chair, her rail-thin body practically trembling. Shoulders squared and head back, she looked like she wished she had stun gun or something. Maybe even a weapon of mass destruction.

Aiden was angry, sure, but there was a part of him that also felt amused. This sort of people, this kind of infighting was what tore most groups apart. It was also the thing that kept them from actually *helping* other people. Such a waste.

It made him even more thankful for the soup kitchen. Thankful for people who realized, even though they had differences and disagreements, that the bottom line was feeding people every day.

There was a tingling in his chest, a sign that the fire was returning. The longer the shouting went on, the more the fire increased. He tried to remember the feeling of Brigid telling him to prepare for battle. And to recall the sense of Her mantle around his shoulders. It helped. His anger slowly morphed into a sense of resolute certainty.

He caught Jaqueline looking between Reverend Laney and himself, eyes darting back and forth. He wondered what that was about. Was she waiting for him to *do* something?

She was.

All of a sudden, he knew. He knew what he had to do.

The story Tobias had told him, as they drank wine in his bed. Brigid's story.

He stood up and held his arms out wide, palms of his hands facing down, the way a person might bless a congregation. It took a while for Reverend Laney and Rabbi Schwartz to even notice. He just stood there, silent, breathing, eyes open, arms outstretched.

Finally the rabbi sputtered to a stop, and the reverend whipped his head around. "What the hell are you doing?"

Power thrummed through Aiden. He was getting used to it by now, and didn't fight it. *Pour through me,* he thought. *Speak through me.*

"I am speaking the truth of the ages. I am calling on the holy fire. I am calling upon those who stand for justice. I am calling upon those who seek love. This quarreling is beneath us. I speak to remind us of the truth of this beloved world."

He inhaled, and it felt as though the whole room inhaled with him. He exhaled, and felt the power of the Holy Spirit moving like a wind. "I call upon each of you here, now, to open your hearts. Open your minds. Call down the holy fire with me. Let's remember why we're here."

Aiden waited. He waited until he felt the spirit settle. He could sense that some people were still fighting it. Like Reverend Laney. He breathed in more deeply and exhaled again. The flame inside of him burned clear and true.

"If serving the houseless is our mission and our mandate, why would we reject any help that comes our way? If we can work together, Catholic, Buddhist, Sikh, Baptist, and Jew, why then would we reject those who come to us in good faith, who practice their own religion?"

Jaqueline was nodding at him. He looked at every face gathered there in the circle, making sure they knew he saw them. He could tell that she saw them too. Brigid. Of course. Brigid.

Reverend Laney spoke again, more quietly this time. "I don't understand how you, a good Catholic, can countenance working with witches."

"I want to tell you all a story I heard just yesterday, when I needed it. It's about St. Brigid."

"We don't have *time* for stories!" Reverend Laney said.

"Hush, please, you've spoken enough," said Dan, from the Episcopal church.

Aiden waited. Reverend Laney and Rabbi Schwartz both sat back down. Then he began, voice taking on the cadence of the storyteller, spinning words into the fluorescent-lit room as though the gathered people sat around a campfire.

"Brigid, it is said, wanted a piece of land for the people. She wanted a place where they could till the soil and feed each other. A place where her sisters could live in community, to worship, and grow strong. But the mayor and the landlords had locked up all the land, and the archbishop was in on it, too."

He paused. "There's a long history of the church and the state working together against the people, you know. Putting money before God and community."

A few people had their arms crossed over their chests. Still not entirely happy. Others looked at him, waiting for him to go on. A few were even nodding. He noticed that on the whiteboard tonight was a quote from the Bible, written in red. *The greatest of these is love.* 1 Corinthians, 13.

"Well, Brigid, she was very clever. She came to the Archbishop and the mayor, and she said, 'I need this land for the people.' They said, 'You cannot have it all, but we can offer you a small gift.' Brigid pretended to think about it. Then she said 'Would you consider giving me the amount of land that will fit beneath my mantle? It is all I need.' The Arch-bishop and the mayor smiled indulgently and laughed. 'Of course we would,' the mayor said, 'Stretch your mantle out on the field and we will mark it for you and that land will be yours to do with as you wish.'

Aiden wished he had some water or tea. His throat was getting dry. But the fire burned on inside him, and the story wasn't done.

"'Very well,' said Brigid, 'you are very gracious and generous men.'"

Aiden could feel that everyone was listening now. He felt Brigid's mantle wrapped around his shoulders. He felt the clear flame burning in his heart.

"Brigid and three of her nuns went to the vast and fertile field. Each took a corner of her green mantle. 'Walk as far as you can, without the mantle ripping or touching the ground,' Brigid said. So the four women set out, walking north, south, east, west, each holding a corner of the mantle in her hand. As they walked, each step of prayer, the mantle stretched and stretched and grew. And they kept walking south and north, west and east, and still the mantle stretched behind them, growing in their hands. And finally Brigid stopped and turned. 'This is enough,' she said. 'This is a goodly parcel, for us to build our home, and for the people to have rich soil to grow their food.' She looked out across the vast acreage to where the mayor and the Arch-bishop were but small dots on the horizon. And she raised her voice, and sounding like the trumpet of God, her voice carried across the green. 'As you have decreed, this is the land that fits beneath my mantle. This land is under my protection now. This land is held for the people of God and we thank you for it.'"

Aiden walked, pacing around the circle, touching the

back of every chair, gripping a shoulder here, touching an outstretched hand there. The spirit was still with him. The spirit was still with the room. He could feel it.

"If Brigid herself, a woman I know as a saint—but that my friend Tobias from the Arrow and Crescent coven tells me is also a Goddess—offers us the example of claiming land for the people, should we not work together to do the same? And if Brigid herself used magic to ease suffering and to challenge the powers and principalities of her day, should we not do the same?"

Rabbi Schwartz stood again, turned toward Aiden, and spoke, "You shame us all, Aiden, and I thank you for it. Thank you for reminding us of the task at hand, and asking us to remember that in order to do God's work, we need to put aside our petty squabbles." She turned to the committee. "But more importantly than that, he reminds us that the primary work of spirit is the work of justice. And if we are to honor a just God, then we should take whatever help comes. I hope everyone here agrees." She sat back down.

Jaqueline stood then. "Thank you, Aiden. And well said, Rabbi. Reverend Laney? Did you have anything you needed to say?"

The Reverend shook his head, mouth tight.

"Then can we all agree, please, that the Arrow and Crescent Coven is invited back? All in favor, please raise your hand."

Every hand in the room except Reverend Laney's reached for the sky.

Aiden bit his tongue. He had said enough. The holy fire was dying down. He didn't trust himself to speak without it. He might rip the reverend's head off.

"Reverend? Are you willing to stand aside?" Jaqueline asked.

"Yes."

Good. Aiden would tell Tobias. And hoped Jaqueline would call the Buddhists, too. And some Sikhs. And maybe that man Arnie from the Wasco tribe that Raquel had mentioned. It was time to get to work.

25

TOBIAS

The circle was cast, and flickering candles on the central altar perfumed the air with the scent of melting beeswax. A tall, pillar candle stood at the very center, and a dark dish filled with water was placed next to it. The white paint on the sloped attic ceiling reflected the candlelight.

Arrow and Crescent were gathered, all nine members, each taking a place in the sacred circle.

Moss and Lucy had called upon Brigid to join them. Tobias felt Her presence like a breath of early spring, caressing his face and massaging his head. It made him feel as though he could start anything. As though all of his angst and worry, all of his fear and sorrow, could become fertile soil for something that was yet to come. He finally felt the possibility of a fresh start.

A beginning.

Some rituals were like that: there was the larger focus, the work the group was doing. Sometimes that felt like the more important work. But there was also the magic that each individual carried into the circle, and that the circle answered back. That was important, too.

Good ritual repaired the fabric of the world. Be it individual, or community. Be it global, or cosmic. The Gods and spirits had their own plans and wishes, as did the earth, and if the human stepped up to meet them—Tobias had been taught by Brenda and Raquel, and every member of this coven—healing could occur, from past to future. He was taught that the present was a fulcrum, and that every moment was a chance to regain the balance that had been lost.

His own balance of fire and earth met the scent of air. *That* was what he brought to circle tonight.

Raquel began to rock and sway on her cushion, dreadlocks swinging out and back moving with her. She held out her hands, left palm facing downward, right palm facing up, receiving and giving, a way of passing blessings around the circle. Tobias matched her swaying. The whole circle, all nine bodies, began to move, rocking like a gentle wave, syncing their breathing, letting their attention deepen.

"Slow your breathing down," Raquel said. Her voice was warm like the flames of the candles, strong and soothing. "Let all your thoughts, your worries, your hopes, your fears, drop down into the stillness in your belly. Breathe deeply. Breathe in the blessings of this coven, the blessings of this night, and the blessings of Brigid herself."

Rocking and swaying, swaying and rocking. Tobias's eyes rolled back in his head he took in a shuddering breath and let go.

"Holy Brigid, holy Brigid, holy Brigid." The words were coming from Tobias's lips, but it felt as though he was not even speaking them. The energy just moved through his lungs, vibrating his vocal cords, and formed words before his mind even thought them.

"Brigid, I pledge to you to forge justice from the fires of love. I'm still working out what that means, but I have a feeling that this work we are called to do here tonight is part of that. I ask you to inform us, to show us the way. I call upon your wisdom. Your powers of healing. And I call upon the strength you imbue in every tool that passes through your forge. Holy Brigid, let us be tools in the hands of love and justice. Let us be shaped to this purpose. So that we may help those who are in greatest need."

This time it was Brenda's voice who picked up the thread. "Send your spirits outward," she told the coven. "Release your spirit from your physical form until together we are flying above the city, our beloved Portland, Oregon. Look at the lights, see the gleaming ribbons of the great Willamette and Columbia Rivers. Gaze on the spans of bridges. Feel the animals, the people, the houses, the cars, the trees and mountains that form this city, the cinder cones and volcanoes that ring it, and feel our connection to each other and our connection to this place."

Tobias breathed deeply, trusting that his physical body took in the air. When he first joined the coven and learned astral journeying, he never knew if he was just pretending or not. What he discovered over the years was that it didn't really matter. The teaching went that imagination, thought, and experience were all intertwined. If something affected you, it made it real. So he trusted now, and let his spirit fly. He opened his inner eye, gazing down upon the city.

After his senses had opened full force that morning, everything looked brighter, and felt stronger, palpable.

He felt the coven around him, all flying. Tugged forward by a calling, a sense of need, he started flying towards downtown. Crossing the Willamette River, he headed to the large encampment in the Pearl District, just north of downtown.

The camp seemed particularly vital and alive. There were many shining dots of humanity all clustered together.

"This is it. This is where we need to make our stand."

He wasn't sure whether or not he had said those words out loud, but he felt the coven respond. They circled the encampment. It was filled with bright colors of the beings who lived there. He could see their auras. Forest green and rich yellow. Purple and orange. Plants and trees, humans and animals. But surrounding the camp was a noxious thread of rusty red and dirty green. Clear colors turned to mud with twisted intentions.

Tobias wasn't sure what those colors were, but just looking at them made him feel slightly sick. Fear and greed could twist the colors of the spirit, he knew. And every city had its own spirit. So did the police. The fire department. Every corporation. Even the city council.

Every group of people formed a spirit together, what some called a "third body" or an "egregore." And they could become just as twisted as an individual. Sometimes even more so, because groups didn't have clarity of conscience.

So, what was rusty red and dirty green? Tobias had a feeling they were going to find out soon, whether on the astral plane, or in the physical, he didn't know.

Brenda's voice cut through the æthers again, joining the physical with the astral plane through sound. "It's time to return. Feel your body tugging at your spirit. Come back home."

Tobias felt himself move rapidly downward. He felt the calling of flesh to spirit, he felt the ways in which they were not separate but one. He eased in through the crown of his head, slipping into his body until he was inhabited from head to toe.

And then Moss spoke. "Brigid, we need to help our houseless brothers and sisters, our siblings who live on the streets, or in shelters, in doorways, under freeways, in tents, or on cardboard in the rain. We ask your blessing for this work. We ask you to guide us. Give us insight. Lend us strength. Let us bring healing and wholeness to our city that is in so much pain. Let us act as protectors for those in need. Brigid, show us how."

Yes.

And then, just as they had done on her feast day a week before, they each stepped forward to gaze into the well and feel the flame. Tobias moved forward with Tempest and Alejandro, and they all bowed their heads toward the fire and water and knelt.

Brigid appeared to him, luminous. It was as though a thousand candles lit her up from the inside. Her skin and eyes glowed with it. She was just as Aiden had described her. The green cloak around her shoulders flew backwards in the wind but the flame in her left hand only flickered and burned more brightly, never to be extinguished. In her other hand she held something very tiny, pinched between two fingers. He couldn't tell what it was. He leaned forward, and smelled sulfur. It tickled the back of his tongue. It was as though he could taste fire.

"Lady, I do not understand."

She held the object higher. He could see it now, just barely. A tiny stick with a red dot at the tip.

Her voice resounded in his head. *You shall become the match that kindles flame.*

26

AIDEN

He had to see Tobias tonight. Aiden felt desperate with the need. That story about Brigid and her mantle...it was working in him. Working through him. He knew they needed to use it somehow. To make things right in this city again, but he had no idea how.

His Catholicism had carried him all these years, even when he almost left it, feeling rejected, it had taken him back into its embrace. But this? This all was something new, and Aiden was no longer certain whether he was dealing with the Goddess, or the Saint.

Does it matter?

He wasn't sure of that anymore, either.

But the story was important, and Tobias would know what was needed. Or maybe the coven would be able to figure something out.

That was another thing: he needed to tell Tobias about the fact that Brigid had been the one to come through for the coven in the end. It was her story that had convinced them, somehow, not anything he had said.

In all his life, Aiden had never known his religion to

work this way. It was freaking him out a little bit. It felt far away from what he was used to, from just going to mass and confession, and saying his prayers at night. It felt too close to what Tobias called magic.

He hadn't liked Tobias joking about that, the night he found out the man he'd slept with was a witch, but he was starting to suspect he was right. All Aiden knew was that his life was turning on its head. Stuff was happening to him that he couldn't explain or understand.

Damn it, he thought, *I was happy just making soup and scrubbing pots.*

He stepped off the bus, navigating the bright streets of the shopping district on Division, skirting past people leaving bars and restaurants, and nodding at a few folks out in front of a café, smoking and talking in the light rainfall. Turning a corner, he entered the darker residential neighborhood, the streetlamps spaced far apart, their light diffused by the shadows of tree branches.

His current tendency to let words just spout from his mouth, coming from nowhere...was just weird. And he wondered now if those Biblical prophets were that different from some of the street people. They came into the kitchen, and sometimes the words sounded like babble, but occasionally, one of them looked at a person, clear-eyed, and delivered a message that carried real weight, and the quality of truth.

He knew more than one person who had a story like that, about the street person stopping their rant, staring right at them, and saying something that caused the hairs to stand up on the back of their neck.

Aiden carried no illusions that he was a prophet, but maybe some of the folks people called crazy were. Who knew? He sure didn't anymore. But maybe battle needed crazy.

Pulling his three-iterations-old phone out of his jacket pocket, he tried calling Tobias again. Still no answer. Right. The coven was working tonight. It was probably rude to just show up on someone's doorstep, probably against some dating code, too, but he didn't care.

Not tonight.

Aiden had caught a bus from downtown to the Richmond district where Tobias and his housemates lived. He needed to tell Tobias what had happened at the meeting, how Brigid's story had come through. He needed to share the holy fire with him.

And now what was he doing? Approaching a dark house. Tobias wasn't home yet. His housemates must be either out or in bed. Aiden could smell the mingled scents of pine and the woodsmoke from a fireplace somewhere in the neighborhood.

His throat was a little tender. He hoped he wasn't coming down with something. That was the last thing he needed. Fishing in his coat pocket, he dug out a packet of lozenges that had been there for months, and popped one in his mouth. Eucalyptus and honey.

Then he sat down, shivering a little, on the front stoop of Tobias's home and watched the steady fall of rain.

It was late. There were barely even any cars coming and going on Tobias's street. No people out walking dogs. Aiden started to second guess himself. Maybe he should have just gone home. At least he'd be warm now. He could be hanging out with Renee and Reggie, Brad, Stingray, Sister Jan, and Ghatso, their resident Buddhist. He could have told them about the stupid arguments on the Interfaith Council. They would be snorting and shaking their heads. Sister Jan would have made him a cup of tea.

He could have talked to them about Brigid. And what had been happening inside of him. He hadn't told them anything, stopping every time he felt the impulse to share.

He knew his housemates—his community—were worried about him. But until tonight, all he could have told them was that he was angry, and that fury compelled him to act. Even if he didn't know why he had to do things like pray in the middle of hailstorms, the anger had compelled him. And he knew saying that would only worry them more.

And a saint appearing to him in the middle of it all? Funny, he'd been able to tell the witch, but not the Catholics.

Tonight, though? Maybe he was ready to come clean. To tell them everything. About collapsing in the church. The saint. The visions. The holy fire.

The air smelled of rosemary and rain. Aiden breathed deeply, trying to clear his head.

He certainly needed to tell them they had to get ready for battle. The stakes had changed, almost overnight. And a bunch of middle-class, middle-aged, petty-squabbling, interfaith people were going to need training in tactics that would make them effective and strong.

The folks from De Porres House who knew how? They were going to need to train up a group of barely willing activists.

This was going to be some undertaking. Aiden hoped that they had time. *He* wasn't trained for battle himself. He knew Stingray and Brad were. And maybe Sister Jan. She'd certainly been arrested before, but that was years ago. He wasn't even sure about the others. Well, they could all learn together, couldn't they?

"Hey. What are you doing here? I thought you were going to text if you were coming by. And you didn't leave a message when you called. Sorry I couldn't pick up, by the way." Tobias was home, heading up the walkway between two bare Japanese maple trees.

Aiden stood up on the porch steps, beneath the dripping eaves, and watched the man he was willing to fight for approach. Tobias's hood was up, but Aiden could see his shadowed face. It was smiling.

Right. He said he would text. He'd completely forgotten that.

"I just...needed to see you."

Tobias climbed the steps, boots thunking on the old wood. Aiden reached for him. Felt the solidness of his body pressed up against him. Felt the damp of his face against his cheek.

"Do you want to come in?" Tobias breathed into his neck.

"Yes, please."

Then Aiden felt his lips, seeking out his own. They were cold, but soft.

Tonight, he tasted like the rain.

27

TOBIAS

"We're going to need to train, is what Aiden said."

Tobias had taken a break from work and walked over to Brenda's shop. Serendipitously, Lucy had also stopped by on her lunch break. They sat in Brenda's back room, eating sandwiches and soup.

Brenda had opened the curtains that divided the classroom and meeting space from the rest of the shop so she could keep an eye and ear out while they ate. It was Tempest's day off, so she didn't have the extra pair of hands.

They sat on mismatched wooden chairs around a big wood drop-leaf table that was tucked against the wall on class nights. Brenda left it open during the day as an extra work table. Quilted banners representing the four elements hung on each wall. Air was pale blue and yellow; Fire, red and orange; Water, teal and royal blue; Earth, purple and rich brown. They brightened up the room, along with the bookcases running along one wall. The other wall held a mini kitchen, with a microwave and the all-important electric kettle for making tea.

Tobias dipped a spoon into the minestrone soup he'd brought for himself and Brenda from the café next door. It wasn't Raquel's soup, but it was pretty good anyway.

"Train how? In what?" Lucy asked. She wore paint-spattered overalls under an equally spattered sweatshirt, sleeves pushed up on her strong brown arms. Her house-painting business was in high demand, and while she had one team that did exteriors during the drier months, winter and spring she focused on her specialty: interiors. She was a master, and her rates reflected it.

"Resistance. How to blockade properly. How to go limp if necessary. Basically, how to stand between cops and the people whose heads they want to bust in."

Lucy raised an eyebrow at that. "Being Latinx, I have enough trouble keeping cops away from my friends and family. You mean to tell me we're going to head into the fray? The whole coven?"

Tobias shrugged. All of this was brand new to him. He'd never been an activist. That was Moss's territory. He was cool with it, of course, but as a healer, he had figured it was more important that he be there for people in the *aftermath* of battle, not in the middle of it.

Brenda set down her half of the turkey sandwich she was splitting with Tobias. "It makes sense to me. Those tools Brigid gave us last night? How many of them were instruments of war? She wasn't handing out hoes and shovels. How many of us got swords or hammers? Lucy, what did she give you again?"

Lucy looked down at her own sandwich with a furrowed brow. Her shoulders slumped.

Then she straightened up in her chair and raised her head again. "Fine. She gave me a damn spear."

Tobias felt like he wanted to apologize. As though he

had brought them to this place. But that was just his old voices talking, the ones that wanted him to feel responsible for everything. The voices that told him he needed to control everything and was always failing at it.

Maybe he would always feel that way, but last night's vision had made it pretty clear that wasn't actually reality. There were larger forces at work here, and there almost always were.

The coven would be relieved to hear he was finally figuring this out. But without the prop of his usual habits, it almost felt as though he was starting from scratch.

What *was* his place? Healing, sure, but Brigid insisted that wasn't all. What did it mean that he had to be a match? He didn't know yet.

Lucy spoke again. "What's the timetable?"

Tobias set his spoon down. "Aiden was very insistent. He wants us to start training right away. Tonight, if possible. Something's really pushing at him. It's halfway scary, halfway cool. The man is really connected. Brigid is talking to him. I think we need to listen to what's coming through."

Brenda looked thoughtful. "That makes sense to me. That travel we did last night? The weird, sickly looking boundary that was pressing in around the camp? It felt like an acute situation to me. As though things could explode at any moment. And the warning from the city council member coming when it did, along with the messages from Brigid? Things are about to catch fire."

Tobias shivered, as though a ghost had walked over his grave. He didn't like her words, but he couldn't deny that they felt true.

But talk of fire when he was the one holding the match? That wasn't resting easily inside him.

"I'll call the rest of the coven," he said. "If we're going to do this, we all have to be in. *All* the way in. I can feel it."

He also knew that he had a formula to make for the city. And he finally knew what herbs he was going to use.

28

AIDEN

I t was actually happening. Too quickly. Too soon.

They needed more time. A month, at least. Even a week would have been better than this. There was no way they were going to be ready for what was coming.

"When is anyone ready for what life throws at them, man?" Barry asked. Aiden startled. He hadn't realized he'd been speaking out loud.

He'd invited Barry and some other folks from his encampment to the interfaith meeting. They needed to be included. Should have been involved all along. But tell middle-class folks that they need to actually work with the poor instead of just giving them clothing and food? Good luck.

Raquel had gotten through to Arnie and he'd brought two other local members of the Wasco nation. They were conferring in a corner, sitting near an upright piano. Arnie was gesturing about something. Looked like the small group was cooking up a plan.

They were gathered in the big church hall tonight. They needed space for Ghatso, Stingray, and Brad to do the training. Moss, from Tobias's coven, had hooked in with those three as well. Apparently he was some sort of activist badass.

The Interfaith Council had grumbled at yet another meeting, and Aiden wasn't sure how many of them would actually show up.

This was the real deal. Getting people to defend a camp? He didn't even know if it was going to work. Maybe it would be like last time: a few of them would show up and the cops would prevail.

The fire inside of him flared. *Not this time.* Not this time.

He looked around the big hall. Stacks of chairs and long folding tables had been cleared to the walls. The space was ready for action. He saw Stingray talking with a couple of pastors and with some of Tobias's coven members. Raquel and Brenda, and a couple of people whose names he couldn't remember.

Stingray looked ready for action, too. Tobias just looked tasty.

A group of Black Bloc activists showed up, in black hoodies, black bandanas over their noses and mouths. They were followed by another anarchist contingent in an assortment of winter coats and jeans, and the local socialist union, many of whom wore red scarves or kerchiefs around their necks.

"Who the fuck invited these people?" said a scratchy voice behind him. *That* was a voice he'd always recognize.

"I'm surprised at your language, Reverend Laney," Jaqueline said. "I asked Aiden's crew to invite them. We need more bodies to pull this off. I know you don't like to get your hands dirty, but these people show up."

She arched one perfectly groomed eyebrow.

"Show up and smash windows," the reverend grumbled.

"Show up and link arms with us," said Stingray, walking toward them through the clumps of people gathering on the white Formica floor of the church hall. She must have heard the rev. He was not exactly a quiet man.

"We about ready here?" Stingray asked Jaqueline. Jaqueline looked a little flustered. Huh. Was she hot for Stingray? Aiden had no idea Jaqueline was even a lesbian. Or he supposed she could be bisexual. Well, well, well. The working-class butch and the business femme. You just never knew about people sometimes.

"Yes. We're just waiting for the Buddhists...and here they are. I'll make an announcement."

Jaqueline walked off, heels of her boots clicking on the floor. She stood in the center of the room and clapped her hands three times.

"May I have your attention, please? Can we all get in close enough to listen. Will some of you bring chairs to the center for folks who need to sit? And make way for the wheelchairs, please."

People rearranged themselves into rough concentric circles around Jaqueline. Some of the older folks—two white men and a Latinx—and a young Asian woman with a cane, sat in chairs. Two wheelchair users rolled up next to them.

"Thank you for coming on such short notice. My name is Jaqueline, and I work for the Unitarian church. We're a disparate group tonight, and I ask that we all set aside our differences and work together. I'd like to introduce Stingray and Ghatso, who will be our main facilitators tonight."

Stingray waved a hand. "Hello folks, I'm Stingray, and this is Ghatso and Brad. We're from De Porres House of Hospitality. Moss from the Arrow and Crescent Coven is helping out, too. What we plan to do here tonight is go through some drills on how to work effectively together when placing ourselves between police and people in danger."

She gestured to some pockets in the circle. "I know some of you here are well trained in civil disobedience. That's part of why you're here. We'll be calling on you to help demonstrate and teach tonight. But before we start, I'd like to ask Barry and some of the other folks from the encampment to explain what the emergency is."

"I'm not comfortable working with people in masks!" a voice called out.

"We're not comfortable working with people who want to unmask us!" one of the Black Bloc activists responded.

Aiden and Jaqueline both stepped forward and held up their hands for quiet. Aiden motioned to her to take the floor.

"I want us all to take a moment. Close your eyes. If you are the praying kind, say a prayer. If you aren't the praying kind, just take a minute to remember what you value."

There was some grumbling, but people actually did as Jaqueline said. After a couple of minutes, she spoke again.

"Thank you. And now, I want us all to remember that we aren't here to fight with one another. We're here for our houseless community members."

"And none of us can do this alone," Barry said. "Those of us who live in Open Heart camp take care of each other as best we can. Sure, we fight, just like you do. Sure, some of us act more responsible, just like you. But the thing is..." He paused. It looked like he was about to cry. He pressed his right hand to his eyes, then blinked.

"The thing is, that at this point, we need more bodies on the line, saying we're important, too." He cleared his throat and waved a hand, indicating he was done.

An Asian woman squeezed Barry's hand. She looked like she was from the camp, too. Barry nodded and opened his mouth again. "The cops have been showing up, harassing us, more and more. They cleared the 205 camp just last week. They could give us twenty-four hours notice at any point, and it's feeling like it's going to be soon. This means we need your help. But if all you're gonna do is argue about who you're going to include, and who is or isn't worth working with? We know where we always end up when the chips are down. We end up in the group you don't like."

The woman spoke then. "We don't want your pity. What we want is for you to stand with us and help us protect our homes."

"Solidarity!" one of the socialists called out.

"Solidarity!" responded the anarchist and Black Bloc contingents.

"That's right," Barry said. "Solidarity." Then he raised a fist in the air.

Stingray raised her fist, too, and stepped back into the center of the circle.

"As Sheila and Barry said, this is an emergency. Anyone not willing to work with every person in this room tonight or tomorrow, please leave now. We are literally down to the wire here and don't have time for anything other than folks wanting to show up."

She waited. No one moved.

"Let's do this," Jaqueline said. "Aiden? Stingray?"

Aiden took a breath, and called upon the holy fire.

"Brigid, if you want us to prepare for battle, please help us now."

Then he went to try help organize and train the most diverse group of people he'd been around in his life.

29

TOBIAS

They hurried from one of the big, multistoried parking lots on the edge between the downtown shopping district and the Pearl, where Open Heart camp was located. Apparently the camp was in an empty lot between the big post office and the railroad tracks. Tobias rarely made it up this far. His usual radius extended only as far as the gay bars that bordered the lower edge of the Pearl.

Downtown was fairly deserted. Most of the office workers had hurried home to dinner already, and frankly, the rain had really started coming down. Even the fancy restaurants and the mall with the movie theater seemed empty.

As usual, they passed some folks sitting on cardboard in the doorways of the fancy shops. Tobias really *saw* them now. He felt a twinge as he realized that for the past several years, he had passed these people by, barely noticing their presence, except to throw the occasional dollar into an outstretched cup.

When Tobias had told Aiden the coven intended to head

to the camp that night, he had recommended they not park too close, in case the cops showed up early and blocked them in.

"It's one thing some of the anarchists talked about after you all left. Don't park in the same neighborhood as the protest."

The training had been intense. Tobias was still sore from it, two nights later. Stingray and her crew, along with several of the anarchists and socialists, had trained them to go limp as they were being dragged away. Raquel had a good insight into that. "Imagine that you are one with the earth beneath you. Your body isn't separate from the earth."

Once she had said that, it had all gone easier for Tobias. They had also linked arms in formation, as others tried to bust through the lines. They'd practiced standing or sitting still and strong while people yelled directly into their faces.

The group had gone over strategies for working with the wheelchair activists, and with some of the folks who had other disabilities. It was all eye-opening. And it gave Tobias something to do with his natural tendency to spark off. Like the herbs, the physical training grounded his impulse toward anger.

He still had no idea what it meant that Brigid had basically handed him a match and told him to start a fire.

"Does the camp know we're coming?" Tempest asked.

"Yes," Tobias replied. "Barry got ahold of Aiden. That's how we got word that the cops gave them the twenty four-hour warning. Once he told me that, I said we'd come down tonight to do some preparation. Aiden said he'd pass the word along."

"You really like the guy, don't you?" Tempest asked.

The Pearl had been an industrial area, and one of the

places near actual services like food, shelters, and medical care where the transient and houseless populations of the city could stay. These days, they were getting squeezed into smaller and smaller areas, as large buildings with expensive lofts, breweries, and boutiques moved in.

Hence the order to disperse and move on. The only question was, where? To a neighborhood an hour and a half bus ride from the nearest free clinic or gospel mission? Even though De Porres House of Hospitality was on the other side of the river in another industrial area, it was still close in, which meant the further people got shoved toward the edges of the city, the less able the community would be to serve them.

"Tobias? You avoiding answering?" she said, poking him in the ribs with an elbow.

"Oh! No. Just...thinking. Yeah. I really like the guy." He smiled. That was only half the truth. He was in love with the man he'd only met just less than two weeks ago. How in the world had everything changed so quickly? Tobias had gone from feeling like he was walking through molasses to feeling like his pants were on fire. He laughed at himself. His pants were on fire in more ways than one.

Luckily, Aiden had decided they needed to have as much sex as possible before the battle began. Tobias was holding off on teasing him about his definition of friendship, figuring he'd just enjoy himself for now.

"Where is this place?" Lucy asked from behind them.

"I think we're almost there," Tobias replied.

Sure enough, there it was, a bright, accordion boundary of painted doors, with cartoon figures, hearts, and "this is our home" painted on them. Some of the Open Heart denizens seemed to be picking the doors up and moving them.

The scene was lit by big, yellow industrial lights from the rail yard.

"What are they doing?" Tempest wondered, as the coven all paused for a moment to regroup and watch.

"Let's find out," Raquel replied, leading the way. She approached a short white man with a limp, who was gesturing to two other people near the doors. "Hi! My name is Raquel. We came by to do some protection work for the camp, if that's okay. Is Barry around?"

"Barry?" the man said. "Yeah, think he's in the center of the camp right now. Follow the doors."

Raquel thanked him and the coven trooped into the camp, following the people carrying the doors away. They skirted through tents and cook stoves and wash stations. Tobias could see a row of portable toilets at the far edge of the camp. He wondered who paid for them.

The camp smelled like soup, coffee, propane, and unwashed socks. Even the rain couldn't wash the cacophony of scent from the air. Camping lanterns cast bright beams here and there among people's homes of dome tents and tarps.

There was Barry, black watch cap on his head, bulky work coat on his big shoulders, in what appeared to be the center of the large camp. He was coordinating something with the doors that looked like the beginnings of a tight spiral.

"Barry!" Raquel shouted. His head jerked up and he smiled.

"Hey! Aiden said you all would be stopping by!"

"What are you doing with the doors?"

"We don't want the cops to trash them, or to tip them over onto people's tents. So we're moving them inside. I thought a spiral might be nice."

Tobias looked at the pattern. It was perfect. The spiral shape was going to help the magic they had planned a lot.

"You're an artist," Tobias said.

Barry raised his right hand and tilted it side to side. "So-so. What do you all need to do here tonight?"

Raquel spoke again. "We want to lay down some protection magic, but first of all, we want to make sure it's okay with the people who live here."

Barry stretched his arms, sweeping the camp. "Everyone here is on board with whatever kind of help you all want to bring. I told them you were cool, and so did Sheila. So, you cool!"

"Can we work with the doors?" Tobias asked.

Barry stopped for a minute, and studied Tobias's face. Tobias wondered how psychic the man was. It was clear he was looking for something. Something not quite physical. Then his eyes changed, focusing clearly again.

"Why you think I'm forming them into a spiral, man? We're open heart. But that doesn't mean we're gonna let the cops traipse through here in a straight line."

The coven laughed. This was definitely Tobias's season of getting his mind blown. Even the homeless camp worked magic in Portland. And why wouldn't they?

"Okay. We'll work with your spiral then," Brenda replied. Her brown hair frizzed out from underneath her coat hood, her face shining in the crosshatching of the camping lanterns and the big industrial railway lights. "Tobias brought some herbs to help the magic. He tells us they're also good for us generally, so we'll all be taking them tonight and tomorrow, before the action."

Tobias swung his messenger bag around to the front and opened the big flap. He showed Barry, and Sheila, who'd shown up to greet them, the small amber bottles.

"It's a mixture I made to help support us as we invoke Justice, Strength, and Love. I figured we'd need those three things to do this, right?"

Sheila nodded. "What herbs are in it?"

"Comfrey, calendula, astragalus, and rose."

"Sounds good. When should we take 'em?"

"We were going to take some now, before we start the magical working, and then planned to take some more tomorrow, right before the action."

Sheila and Barry started calling people over. He passed the bottles out, explaining what they were. He passed a bottle to Moss, so the coven could start dosing with the herbs. When he turned back from giving out all the bottles he had brought, he almost burst into tears.

It was so beautiful. Usually, people raised the dropper and squirted the herbs into their own mouths. That wasn't what was happening here. People seemed to be saying a prayer, then raising the dropper for their friends, who, heads tilted back, faces wet with rain, received the herbs on their tongues.

Tobias wished Aiden was there. It looked an awful lot like how people described communion.

There was magic every damn where.

"Tobias?" Alejandro stood in front of him in his fancy leather hat and long raincoat. He held the dropper up, a questioning look on his face. Tobias tilted back his head and stuck out his tongue.

The rain felt like a blessing. The herbs were tart, a cascade of flavors running toward the back of his mouth.

"Thanks, man."

The whole thing took longer than Tobias expected. He had thought people would just take the bottles and head off to their separate camps, but everyone wanted to do this, all at once. So they waited in the rain.

Tobias found that he didn't mind. He could feel the magic deepening around them, starting to radiate out from the growing spiral of doors. People had been continuously bringing them in during the ceremony, placing a door into the pattern, then pausing to receive some of the formula.

"Strength, justice, love." Brenda and Raquel began speaking the words in a rhythm, like a chant. "Strength, justice, love. Strength, justice, love."

The chant rippled out, the coven walked the spiral of the doors, touching each door, imbuing it with the magic of protection. There was no need here to call the elements and form a sphere. The people who lived here were already doing it. The elements were all around them, every day. The ground beneath their feet, the fires of their propane stoves, the air in their voices, and the water falling from the clouds above.

They formed a procession, spiraling out to the edges of the camp. When they reached each corner, Brenda and Raquel touched the ground there, and then raised the energy to the sky. Every person walking with them did the same. And so they went, corner to corner, until they had walked the edges of the camp.

Tobias felt a woman slip her hand into his. He held out his hand to the man next to him. People grabbed hands, or grasped shoulders, until everyone was touching someone else.

"Let this place be a holy place! Let this holy place be a safe place! May the people here be strong! May the people here remain community! May the people here be safe, and joyous, healthy and whole!" Raquel's voice filled the sky, rising through the pouring rain.

"Strength! Justice! Love!" the people started up the chant again—"Strength! Justice! Love! Strength! Justice! Love! Strength! Justice! Love!"—until everyone who could was dancing in the rain.

"So mote it be," Tobias whispered to the sky. "So mote it be."

30

AIDEN

The council chambers were packed. The seats downstairs were all full, and people stood at the back. Aiden was up on the round balcony that skirted the room. There were families there—Black, white, and Latinx—and the Asian Seniors Coalition was downstairs, along with the Homeless Health van people. And everyone from De Porres House, of course, including volunteers and guests.

The Portland City Council had tried to pull a fast one and shifted their regular morning meeting to evening. But a little bird named Terry Benson had tipped Aiden off. And Aiden had called in reinforcements. He'd contacted Friends and Family, the free restaurant downtown, and notified the two gospel missions, too. He'd also let Stop Shooting Us Now know, and the Bread and Roses Anarchist Collective, and asked everyone to spread the word.

Everyone, it seemed, had decided to let the city council know, since they'd been so kind to have *finally* met after most folks got off work, that they would show up and be good, engaged citizens.

Aiden looked at the big arch-framed mural of Oregon

trees and sky. It felt right to be here. He knew Tobias and his coven were out at Open Heart camp tonight. He felt the warm thrum of connection between his own heart and Tobias's. It gave him hope that tomorrow would go okay, and that whatever this thing Tobias and he were hurtling toward together was going to end up being good, too. Explosive, maybe. But good.

The five commissioners that made up the current city council entered the room. Two women and three men. Two African American members, the other three white. They took their seats behind the long, curved desk. Each seat had a small microphone in front of it. They set down bottles of water, and pulled out tablets or legal pads.

At least half of the council members did not look pleased. The other half? Looked like cats that had just polished off large bowls of cream.

"Stop the sweeps!" a voice from behind him yelled.

"Stop the sweeps!" responded a few voices from downstairs.

One of the white men, commissioner John Johnson,— yeah, that was actually the man's name—leaned into his microphone. "If you insist upon shouting, you may be removed from the council room."

"Fuck you!" a woman yelled.

"Please. I need to call this session to order." Johnson's face was shading into the darker reds. Any minute now, Aiden expected him to start pounding on the desktop, or foaming at the mouth.

Aiden glanced at Benson. Hands clasped neatly in front of her on the swathe of rosewood desk, her curls and lipstick were perfect. She was stifling a smile.

Johnson asked for the agenda and read it out as it flashed on the screen directly above the curved desk, beneath the mural of the trees. Aiden supposed the screen was helpful for those who were hard of hearing, or couldn't see so well, but it sure was ugly, marring the beautiful old chambers.

The council agenda was long and boring. He glanced toward the bottom and saw that, of course, dealing with "homeless camps" was at the bottom. He hadn't even bothered to get a ticket to speak. Let other people stand in line for their five minutes. There were people more deserving of the time, like the actual houseless folks here, and other people far more eloquent than he was. He would sit in the balcony, and bear witness, and pray.

"St. Brigid, are you there?" he whispered. He felt the warmth of wool around his shoulders, and smelled wet grass. Closing his eyes, he let the sounds and scents of the council chambers fall away, and focused only on his memory of Her, and the feel of the mantle, and the scent of green grass.

His head felt light. Literally light. Not light like a balloon, but light as though there were a warm bulb just behind his head. *What, you think you have a halo now?* he thought. Then he felt Her touch on his shoulder, and let the thought go.

A hand on his shoulder. A hand on the crown of his head. A hand touching his heart. A light touch sweeping his brow. Her hands moved around him, like tiny birds, or tongues of flame.

Whoosh! At the thought of fire, the candle in his heart ignited, burning up his chest. Every muscle in his body tensed so hard he shook from the power of it, a spasming rictus that was making it hard to breathe.

"Sir! Are you okay? Sir!" Hands, physical hands now, touching him, surrounding him, trying to get him to lie down. He didn't want to lie down. He wanted to stand up. He needed to stand. He needed air. He needed to see.

Aiden opened his eyes onto the huddle of worried faces above him. He could hear the drone of the city council members down below, and some muffled shouting.

He pushed the hands and shoulders away.

"No. Please. Get off me!"

He shoved his way back up into a sitting position, and leaned hard on the bench in front of him, levering up to his feet.

"Let me through, please. Let me through." He shoved past the people next to him. He had to get to the railing at the front of the balcony. He needed to *see*.

The sky on the painting of the mural had been blue, but was now darkening. The clouds were tinged with undertones of purple and black, lit by the light of a setting sun. What was happening?

Every molecule inside of him was on fire again. Her fire. He saw a vision of a city laid to waste. A city in rubble, decimated by fires and wrecking balls, torched by riots and greed.

Leaning over the metal railing that separated the balcony from the open air above the chambers, Aiden screamed.

Every head snapped upward. He lifted both his arms into the air, and began to sway. Hands grabbed him from behind. His elbow struck something soft. The hands let go.

"You. Must. Stop." Murmurs and whispers and shouts of *What's happening?* erupted in the air. But not from the council members. They were riveted. Staring upward. They couldn't take their eyes from his face. Good.

Okay, Brigid. Tell me what to say. The fire burst from his head, his eyes, his tongue. And then the words came.

"This city, beloved of the smallest rose bush to the tallest, oldest pines, from the rivers to the cinder cones, this city is in danger. This city is in danger of losing its soul. And it is all because of you."

He pointed one long finger at the curved desk of commissioners. Their faces were made of stone, set in anger, bewilderment, or fear.

"You have allowed those who wish to only profit from the lives of all who make this city home hold sway. You have allowed development without heart. You have asked for money and not asked where food or dancing comes from. You are complicit in the rape of the land, the ouster of families from their homes, and the further bleaching of diversity from our communities. You are complicit in the might of the police force, and use them as weapons against the very people they say that they protect."

He was sweating now. It streamed in great rivers down his face and back. Aiden could tell there was movement around him, and people talking, but he was too filled with fire to pay any attention to anything but Her words. His words. Someone's words.

"The death of Mary Jo Sullivan is on your heads. She froze to death because of you. Everyone from 205 camp who is now truly homeless is your responsibility. The lives of every person at Open Heart camp, currently struggling to save their home, are in your hands."

Hands grabbed him from behind again. Rough hands. Aiden tried to elbow them, but hit something hard. He tried to roll his shoulders, shake them off. The hands gripped harder. Someone was trying to force his arms down. He fought to keep them raised.

"Turn from your lives of greed and embrace the light of

love. There is nothing for you but ash and ruin if you continue on your course!"

His arms were yanked behind him. He felt the click of cold steel around his wrists. Arms jerking the cuffs up, pulling on his shoulders.

"Aiden!" He could hear Stingray call his name, but he couldn't see her. Didn't know where she was. "We'll follow you to jail!"

Jail?

"I call down the holy fire upon every person here. Those whom it must bless, shall it bless. Those whom it must curse, so shall it curse!"

"Let's go, buddy." An arm slung him around. He slammed into body armor. It was the same cop who had pushed him down under the freeway, smashing his head.

"This city shall be a refuge of love!" he shouted as loudly as he could, vocal cords threatening to snap. "Bow your heads to love!"

An officer on each arm yanked him away from the edge. He stumbled up the balcony steps.

"I call down the holy fire! There shall be no release for you unless you vow to change! Reward not greed, seek only justice! Embrace the power of love!"

"Shut up," one of the cops said.

People chanted and screaming around him. "Stop the sweeps! Let him go! Stop the sweeps! Let him go!"

The police dragged him through the balcony doors.

And Aiden fainted.

31

TOBIAS

It was the night of the waxing crescent. Though Tobias couldn't see the moon through the clouds and rain, he could feel it. The time of the waxing crescent was a good time for magic. It held the energy of renewal.

Gods and Goddesses knew, Portland needed it.

He was at Pioneer Square, the brick plaza that took up one city block in the heart of downtown, and was a favorite meeting spot for rallies, memorials, and protests, along with book fairs and other cultural events.

Three hundred people gathered around him, standing in the softly falling rain and winter darkness. Concentric circles filled the plaza, cascading up the steps that formed a partial amphitheater. There were no candles. The call had recommended no banners or signs, but some groups had them anyway. Some were clever and had taped slogans onto rain ponchos, or carried their signs like sandwich boards, strung over shoulders or necks.

Mostly, though? The people had just brought themselves—willing bodies and hearts—just as they'd been asked.

Tobias was surprised to find that he recognized a lot of contingents, though others he only identified by their banners. Bread and Roses Anarchist Collective were there. So was the Portland Socialist Society. A group of Catholic nuns. Folks from the Interfaith Council. Don't Shoot Us Now. Some Black Bloc-ers. Buddhists. Africans United. Pacific Islander Student Union. A small contingent from the Sikh temple. And just random folks. Adults from everywhere, it seemed. All of them willing to come out in the rain to help a bunch of houseless people save their homes.

So many communities, all gathered, facing the center of the square. Waiting. Ready to march. The only thing missing were children. There were just no guarantees that anyone out tonight would remain safe, so the call had also asked that children be left at home.

"They came," Brenda said softly, putting an arm around his waist.

"They did." Tobias squeezed her back. "I can't believe this many people came at such short notice. It's beautiful."

The coven surrounded him. The rest of the Interfaith Council was all present, wearing raincoats, hats, and hoods. Some held umbrellas for those who needed them. They would be stashed in vehicles along the way. Once they got to the encampment, they needed freedom to move.

A few of the wheelchairs had umbrellas or small tarps rigged overhead. Smart.

Everyone was there.

Except for Aiden. Tobias felt his absence with a pang, but he was also proud that this man he'd grown to love so quickly had risked himself and gone to jail. The story had spread like torch fire.

Aiden had gone full-on prophet and cursed the city council.

"Cursed them with love," Stingray had said.

"You ready?" Brenda again. Right. He was supposed to kick this whole thing off, and wasn't that strange? After the fight Aiden and Jaqueline had gone through to get the council to accept Arrow and Crescent at all, and they'd chosen to have a witch say the opening prayer.

He didn't know who was responsible for that, but if Aiden couldn't be here to do it, it felt right all the same.

Tobias took a deep breath and stepped into the center of the circle. He began to slowly rotate, face tilted upward to the gray skies, and the darkness, and the falling rain.

He swallowed, then took in another breath, braced his diaphragm muscle to raise his voice, and prayed. "Holy Brigid! Be with us! Guide us. Please. Be with the people gathered here. Be with the people of Open Heart camp. Guide us all. Walk with us. Bless us."

He held up a bag of tincture bottles. "And bless these herbs. May they heal our bodies and strengthen our souls."

He passed the bag to Moss, who distributed them to the rest of the coven. They would offer the herbs to whomever wanted them.

"Send to us the spirit that connects us all. Kindle our hearts with the fires of justice! Let us become, together, a people guided by the power of love. Blessed be."

"Amen!" Rabbi Schwartz spoke loudly from across the circle. Her voice was echoed by others.

"Creator!" the rabbi said. "Forgive us for not caring enough. Help us to care more. Help us to care better. Let us walk in the footsteps of all who have walked the ways of justice. May we lead the way for those who are yet to come. Bless this congregation. Amen."

Stingray, Brad, Sheila, and Barry all came forward at that point.

Brad handed Barry the mic to a bullhorn. The big man held the small box up to his mouth as Brad pointed the mouth of the bullhorn above people's heads.

"My name is Barry, and this is Sheila. We're both part of the Open Heart community. We're an encampment up by Naito Parkway, and our community is in danger. Thank you for coming out tonight. We need you. We also want you to know that if you ever need us, we'll be there. Now Stingray and Brad are going to set some ground rules for tonight's action."

Stingray took the mic.

"Power to the people!" she shouted. "Okay! There are two main things to remember tonight: stay together, and keep calm. We don't know what's going to happen tonight, but the cops may provoke us, or use chemical weapons on us, or even beat us. We hope none of that will happen. And we've got a lot of folks in clergy robes and collars to try to help steer things that way. It's bad publicity for the city if nuns get clocked in the head by police."

There were a few chuckles at that, but also quite a lot of grimaces.

"When we get to the camp, we ask that you listen to the folks from the Interfaith Council, Bread and Roses, Portland Socialists, Don't Shoot Us Now, and De Porres House. All of these people have been at meetings and know the plan. I am *not* going to shout that plan out into the open air tonight! Just know that it is a simple plan, and we're going to keep you all as safe as we possibly can. Okay? Great. Thank you. We'd now like to ask the Wasco and Grand Ronde Nations to bless this march and lead us to the camp."

Led by Arnie, a small contingent came to the center, including four men carrying a huge drum. Two other men had beaters with round skin heads. A woman burned sweetgrass as Arnie raised his arms to each of the four directions. Then the drummers started up a rhythm and began to chant.

Tobias realized that these people from the first nations of this land should have started off the prayers. It was only right. They were on their land. He hadn't thought of it because it was decided they would start the march. But now he felt the wrongness of it. He hoped it didn't affect the magic badly, to have made such a mistake.

He tried to let the sense of worry go. There was too much to keep track of tonight, and he needed to be on point. The bottles of tincture were still being passed around, in an echo of last night's communion. He missed Aiden again. He hoped he was okay. When they told Tobias that Aiden had fainted, he almost rushed down to the jail to break him out. Stingray insisted he wouldn't be of any help, and that two workers from their community would make sure he was taken care of, and meet him when he was released.

Tobias wanted to be there when Aiden got out.

"He'll want you at the camp, Tobias," Stingray said. "Don't you think? He'll want all of us out there who can be. The last thing that would make Aiden feel good would be the thought that he'd pulled a bunch of key people away from the action he helped organize."

Then she surprised Tobias by pulling him into a hug. "He's going through a strange time right now, and I have no fucking idea what happened when he cracked his head on that rock, but I think you're good for him."

Tobias hoped so. He wanted to be.

The drummers were moving, followed by a row of Buddhists, some of them carrying gongs that sounded as an occasional counterpoint to the drumming.

The crowd streamed out of the plaza onto 6th, heading

north, toward the spot where the Willamette curved in its banks, heading northwest only to curve again to meet up with the Columbia.

They were heading for the camp.

"We're on our way, Aiden," he said. "Wish you were here."

32

AIDEN

Aiden's head felt as though someone had short circuited his brain cells. Or as if a lightbulb had exploded inside his head. It ached, and hummed, and flashed. The headache was a ferocious, pounding, stalking animal, rattling its cage.

His body felt battered again. Weary. All it wanted was rest.

But the work wasn't done. Aiden knew it. But there was no pressure inside of him. The incandescent flame had settled, and steadied to a warm glow. No matter what was to come, he had done all that he could.

Aiden felt completely at peace.

The pain in his body was nothing compared to the sense of love and well-being he felt inside his soul. The wrenched shoulders and throbbing lower back were just fine with him. So was the pain in his knees from the concrete floor.

Aiden blessed it all.

He blessed the buzz of the long, fluorescent tube in its cage. He blessed the steel bars and the seatless steel toilet bowl. He blessed the metal sink. He blessed the stink of bleach and vomit, and the stench of the dried sweat brought on by drugs or fear.

He blessed the other inmates, those who were in their own kinds of pain, those who tried to sleep, those who scowled and those who cried.

Aiden was a man of flesh and light.

The edges of his skin felt as if they might just float away. He was buoyant.

He was in a state of grace, and Brigid was with him.

He'd woken up in the city jail, bewildered at first as to what had happened and how he'd gotten there. Once his senses returned, and his brain started functioning again, he soon settled in, knowing that this, too, was part of the service he'd been called upon to offer.

The most beautiful thing about it all? His rage was gone. No more anger. No more fury. Just the certainty that he was loved: by Brigid, by his community, and by a beautiful man named Tobias. No matter what happened, from now on, Aiden would never feel alone.

I am here. And she was. He could see her, standing before him once again. She held a white cloth in her hands, and ran it across his face, salving the bruises where his cheek and chin must have hit the marble floor. The cloth felt warm. Damp. It eased the aching, just a bit.

Time would do the rest.

And then the cloth was gone.

The saint floated, two feet above the stinking concrete floor, green cloak billowing around her tunic. In her hands now appeared a chalice and a burning torch. In her hands were a sword and a scythe. In her arms appeared a bleating lamb. In her hands were a loaf of bread and a mug of beer. In her hands were a bowl of fresh milk.

"What is all this?" he asked her. The images were beautiful, but they made no sense to him.

You can choose, she said.

Ah. Gifts. Weapons. Powers.

He chose the torch.

So you can illuminate and See.

She touched his forehead with her lips. Just a breath. A whisper. And then She was gone.

Aiden held a torch in his right hand.

In the torchlight, among the stink of chemicals and men, among the sound of fearful raving and the clang of bars, he Saw.

The sky above was dark, and full of rain. The flame of the torch in his hand flared and flickered, but would not be doused.

He looked down.

Aiden saw a stream of people, marching, moving steadily toward a river. He saw Tobias, face fierce and beautiful. He saw Stingray and Ghatso, Barry, Sheila, Jaqueline. The reverend and the rabbi. And, toward the curving ribbon of water, he saw a web of brightness, and a spiraling of gates.

The mighty stream of people were headed there. Steadily. Surely. Guided by the heartbeat of a drum.

33

TOBIAS

They reached the camp, and the people living there greeted them. Nothing was cooking on propane stoves tonight. Everything that could be packed away, was. The domed tents remained. Defiant. A sign to all that this place was home.

There was a sense of excitement and tension in the air. Tobias softened the edges of his aura, cast his attention outward, and *felt*. The protections were holding. The camp and its people felt strong.

Good.

A woman ran up and stopped, doubled over her knees, panting out her message. Cops in riot gear were massing, two blocks away. Text messages went out, phones buzzing in pockets. The word spread.

Tobias found he didn't really care. Nothing could make him feel afraid. Not tonight. Tonight, the plants were moving through his bloodstream. He was filled with justice, strength, and love. Nothing could stop him. Not even a truncheon to the head.

He breathed in the rain and the night, and as he

exhaled, sent a breath to the edges of his energy field, sealing his aura once again. He would need a strong container tonight. It would help him remain centered.

Arnie led the men carrying the big drum toward the spiral of doors, heading for the heart of the camp. The beaters kept on with the rhythm, steady and true. He didn't know how they managed, but they never missed a beat. The sound of their chanting faded in and out as they entered the spiraling pathway.

Tobias wondered what was at the heart of those brightly colored doors. He realized he hadn't asked to see.

Perhaps Open Heart camp had its own secrets. That was okay. Every person and place did. Mystery helped keep the spirit alive.

The marching people streamed around the edges of the camp, preparing to surround it. He could feel the drum as it continued on its walk to the center of the the spiraling doors, and felt the energy begin to roll out from the center toward the edges, connecting to the blessed quarters in the corners. Air, Fire, Water, Earth. Above, Below, and Center. The sacred sphere was here. Activated.

The power of the people was part and parcel of the power that rotated Earth upon its axis, and sent it spinning around the sun, a dance that mirrored the spiral of galaxies, and the unfurling of flowers come dawn.

All things wound in and out. Every circle was complete, until it wasn't. But the thing about life? he realized. There was always another phase, a second chance. Even death brought something new to bear.

The sound of boots on tarmac joined the sound of the big drum. The cops were coming, jogging in formation.

He'd better start getting his own people into position. Looking down the line, he saw that, just as planned, members of the Interfaith Council, Bread and Roses, and all the others, were interspersing themselves among the other people who had felt the call and shown up tonight.

"Let's line up, facing out," he said to everyone within reach of his voice. "Link arms. Don't let go. No matter what happens. If you feel scared or unsafe, the time to move is now. Head toward the sound of the drum. Go to the center of the spiral. There's more protection there. Wheelchairs? Your choice. You can stay with us in the line, or help shore up the protections in the center."

No one in his group was leaving. Tobias's heart pounded in his chest, and, not for the first time that night, he felt his throat close up, and his eyes filled up with tears. Every face within hearing distance was trained on him, waiting for further instruction.

He sniffed and cleared his throat, then stood a little taller.

"Okay. Get ready to link arms. We're forming a circle of love and protection around this encampment. If I shout 'down!' we all kneel or sit on the ground or in our chairs. Sitting is more stable and you'll be comfortable longer. Remember, the earth is your friend. Call on earth and she will hold you. Think of gravity like a lover who doesn't want you to leave his bed."

People smiled, faces damp with rain.

"The main thing is, don't let go of the people next to you. Solidarity is the reason we're all here tonight, and solidarity is the only thing that's going to keep us safe and alive, and protect this encampment."

He looked at the people. Men. Women. Those who were neither or both. Black. White. Asian. Latinx. Some with bandanas wrapped around their faces, others in ponchos, or rain hats, or hooded coats. And he loved them. Every single one of them.

"One more thing," he said. "You're all beautiful."

"*We're* all beautiful," said a voice behind a black bandana.

Tobias smiled. "Right. Okay, let's link up. For Open Heart!"

"For Open Heart!"

He slipped an arm into a crooked elbow on his right side and felt an arm slip through his own crooked arm on the left. He held his own hands, and encouraged the people next to him to do the same. He felt the line tighten up around him as the word got passed.

The ground felt sturdy underneath his boots. He could feel Arrow and Crescent in their spots around the perimeter. And, if he softened his awareness, just enough, he could feel Aiden somewhere to the north. It felt like he was smiling.

The rain continued to fall, like a blessing, as the riot cops arrived.

34

AIDEN

S he was everywhere. He could see everything. Brigid was with him in the cell that flickered in and out of his consciousness.

He heard a guard call his name, but couldn't respond. He heard someone else reply, "Just leave him. He's nuts."

His torch illuminated the faces of the men he shared this cell with. They gave him his space. He felt as though the men had cleared a circle around him, allowing him to pray undisturbed, arms outstretched.

Even the raving men had quieted down.

The torch illuminated all. Every person rested in its light.

Except those it was meant to expose.

Aiden saw them, too. He saw the mayor in his office, manicured fingers massaging his temples, bottle of ibuprofen on the desk next to a glass of water. He was moaning.

He saw the city council members, choking down their dinners, snapping at wives, husbands, children, or drinking alone in the gleaming shadows of a bar. He saw a few other people, meeting together in Terry Benson's living room. Sharing a bottle of wine, serious looks on their faces.

Aiden saw himself, body swaying over his knees, surrounded by a group of men. The bars just fell away. They didn't matter anymore.

Aiden saw that the stream of marching people had become a mighty fortress, a beautiful wall. He saw them holding to each other. He felt the spiral, the energy of it swirling in and out. The four corners, holding down the space. Anchoring the people to the land.

He saw plexiglass shields. He heard the pounding of the drum and the discordant, unmatched cacophony of riot sticks on shields. He saw visors, padded gloves.

He felt the fear. The boredom. The disgust. The anger at being out, again, in pouring rain, guarding a bunch of goddamned anarchists and hippies.

He felt the scratch of warm wool around his shoulders. Had one of the men placed a blanket there? Or was it Her mantle, once again? Or both?

Her mantle.

The four corners of the square.

A piece of land...

Secured forever for the people.

"Holy Brigid!" he cried to the night. "Holy Brigid! Unfurl your mantle! Protect the people! Guard the land!"

35

TOBIAS

F ury rolled off the cops. They stood, feet apart, shoulders squared behind their shields, and beat those shields with big black sticks. Tobias couldn't see their eyes behind the visors and the rain. But he knew they were looking. He just wasn't sure what was looking out from behind those eyes. It felt malevolent, not quite human. Or was it?

Human nature could be twisted into anything, he knew. Look at the bravery around him. The people stood, or sat in wheelchairs, arms linked, not letting go.

Not giving up or giving in, even as the cops beat their shields and the pounding grew louder than the big drum in the center of the spiral. Louder than the rain.

Not giving up or giving in, even as the line of cops took one step forward, then another.

It was hard to not lean back, or take a step. But Tobias stood firm, and so did those around him.

The sound of sticks on shields stopped so suddenly, Tobias almost collapsed forward, as if the sound had been holding him upright. The person on his left caught him, patting his back, then linked their arm again. Tobias nodded his thanks.

A tinny, recorded, quasi-feminine voice blared out into the night. "This is an unlawful assembly. Anyone remaining in the area in five minutes will be subject to arrest."

"Down!" Tobias shouted. He felt the line around him struggling to sit and still remain connected. It was a vulnerable moment, but remaining standing was more vulnerable, still. At least this way, it was going to look worse for the cops. Sitting protestors could not easily be painted as inciting a riot.

He saw a flash go off. What was that? He hoped it was just a camera. They hadn't contacted the news, because a lot of the folks in the gathering didn't trust them. Plus, the less they telegraphed to the police, the better.

But scanners were a tool of every reporter. More flashes went off, the light refracted through the rain. Yep. The press had arrived.

The police lowered gas masks and face plates.

"We! Are! A Law-ful Assembly! We! Are! The Open Heart!"

Tobias couldn't tell where the chant had come from, but it was a good one. He joined in, raising his voice with the people next to him, drowning out the tinny, pre-recorded voice.

"This is an unlawful assembly..."

"We! Are! A Law-ful Assembly! We! Are! The Open Heart!"

There was a hiss and something flew past Tobias's head. The acrid, choking scent of teargas. He closed his eyes and held his breath, and wished he had a bandana over his face. He put his hands up to his eyes, arms still linked, and hoped the people next to him were doing the same.

There was no chanting now. So Tobias started to pray.

Holy Brigid, be with the people. Work with us. Guide us. Through the taste of the chemical gas, the ghost of the herbal tincture emerged. Right. The herbs were still swirling in his bloodstream. The plants were doing their work. *Love. Strength. Justice.* The words became a mantra in his head.

"This is an unlawful assembly. Anyone remaining in the area in five minutes will be subject to arrest."

Love. Strength. Justice.

The rain washed the gasses away, sent the poison streaming toward the ground.

:You are a healer. What is needed here?:

Tobias coughed, the acrid gas still burning his lungs. What did it mean to be a healer? He closed his eyes for a moment, listening to the pulse of everything around him. The people. The trees. The railroad tracks. The drumming. The rain.

Healing started with the simplest ingredients. A plant. A breath. An intention. Some love.

What was needed here? The people surrounding the encampment needed to feel this all was worth it. The people needed prayer. And he needed, after years of alternately avoiding and defying his father's wrath, to simply become himself.

A witch. A healer. And a dedicant of Brigid. Goddess of healing. Goddess of the forge.

A hammer blow of thunder rumbled a warning. Five seconds later, lightning cracked the sky.

She was here. Tobias raised his head to the storm and cried out:

"Holy Brigid! Grant us the powers of love, justice, and strength! Holy Brigid, be here now!"

He saw a cop step up behind the line of police in riot

gear that faced the sitting and kneeling community. The
man raised a canister, sending out a streaming jet of red
liquid.

"Duck!" Tobias got out, jerking his head down as the
pepper spray hit his abused eyes, skin, nose, and throat. It
felt as though his whole face was on fire.

:Be the match:, her voice said in his head. It was clear as a
bell ringing in a summer's sky. *:Be the match.:*

Tobias lifted his face again, swollen eyes closed, and let
the rain wash the capsaicin concentration from his skin. It
was going to take more than water to diffuse the burning
oils, but the rain helped.

:Open your eyes.:

He didn't want to. His *eyelids* didn't want to. By sheer
force of will, he opened his eyes, just slits at first, prying
them open as wide as they would go, staring straight up into
the deluge coming down from the sky.

He could hear people around him muttering and groaning. He needed to help them. He couldn't let these bastards
win. He couldn't let the city council, and the mayor, and the
cops, and whatever other greedy fucks were in charge of this
mess take the people down.

:Be a healer. Be the match.:

He swallowed. It felt like shards of glass scraped at his
throat. He knew that everyone next to him felt the same way.
And he had taken on a leadership role, so...

"This little light of mine..." His voice was barely audible.
A whisper in the rain. He cleared his throat. Gods, that hurt.
Damn it.

He kept his face up, letting the rain pour down, but
closed his swollen eyes. He couldn't stand the pain anymore.

Tobias tried again.

"I'm gonna let it shine!" Better. Louder. He felt the man on his right squeeze his arm.

"This little light of mine, I'm gonna let it shine! Let it shine, let it shine, let it shine!" More voices joined in, synching with the drum that still pounded out the heartbeat from the center of the spiraling doors.

Tobias knew there were verses, but it was all he could do to hang on to the refrain, so he just sang it over and over again, forcing air through his abused throat.

"This little light of mine, I'm gonna let it shine..."

He could hear the chant, delayed by space and time, making its way around the circle. He could hear people behind him joining in. People from the camp who hadn't joined the front line were coming closer, singing loudly.

Two officers pushed through the line of riot cops and barreled toward the seated, linked armed comrades. The people sang on.

Two sets of gloved hands grabbed Tobias, ripping at his arms. A face plate smashed into his skull.

36

AIDEN

"Brigid! Tobias!" Aiden screamed.

"Hush man, you're okay." That was a voice from the jail. At least Aiden thought so. He waved it away.

Dropped deeper into prayer.

Something bad was happening. The people were strong, but the flickering, muddy bands around them were stronger. Things were very, very bad.

Aiden held the torch up higher, tried to See.

I am here. That waft of cool and green again. The safe comfort of green wool.

Anchor it to the corners.

He saw what She meant then. She was saying yes, she would do it. She would spread her mantle over the land.

"Grab a corner!" he yelled out.

"What?"

"Grab a corner!"

He opened his eyes and saw a skinny black man crouching down, a concerned look on his face. "You okay, holy man? We've been trying to give you space, but..."

"The blanket! Grab a corner."

Aiden felt around, and sure enough, one of the men had draped his shoulders in a rough gray blanket. He took one corner, and held another corner out to the man. "Take a corner."

The man looked confused.

"Please?"

The man nodded and held on.

"Two more!"

"C'mon, help the holy man out."

Two other men stepped forward, one white and towering, another Black and barrel-shaped. Once all four corners were gripped tightly, Aiden spoke. "Stretch it out. All four corners."

The men stepped away from each other in the thirteen by thirteen cell. It was barely large enough for the number of men being held. The other men shuffled out of the way, crowding together. Then, one by one, each of them grabbed a section of the ratty blanket, until the whole piece of gray fabric was held around the edges by the hands of men.

North. South. East. West. The men stretched the thin gray blanket, shot through with threads of salmon and pale blue, until it couldn't stretch anymore.

"Hold it. Please. Just like that. I'm trying to help some people."

"Whatever you need, holy man. We'll stand right here."

"And we got no place else to go," someone else murmured.

Aiden closed his eyes, and, gripping the blanket with his left hand, held the torch up with his right.

He couldn't tell if the cops still had Tobias. He felt the roiling, angry threads tightening around the sacred land. He heard the heartbeat, drumming in the center.

He heard the song of light. He felt it then.

Brigid unfurled her mantle. It floating out and out and out. It stretched up and down. It stretched toward the river. It stretched toward the Naito Parkway and the rail yards. It reached out to the Steel Bridge and the Broadway Bridge.

He felt the people lift their hands up to the sky, and tug it down.

It was anchored to the people. It was anchored to the land. It was anchored by the water and every pin in every bridge.

Brigid had claimed the land.

And the land was for the people.

37

TOBIAS

The people holding Tobias's arms starting yelling, screaming, "Let him go! Let him go!" The police pulled. Tobias's comrades pulled back. The whole line leaned away from the police, as if Tobias was the center of the rope in a game of tug-o-war.

"This. Little. Light of mine! I'm gonna! Let it shine!" Tobias half yelled, half panted the words. His head ached from where the cop's helmet had smacked him, and despite the rain, his skin felt as if it were on fire.

"Let him go! Let him go!"

"Let it shine, let it shine, let it shine!"

The rain pounded, the drumbeat was strong. The people sang. The police pulled. Tobias felt like his arms were on fire. It was hard not to grit his teeth or yell.

:Be a match.:

Then he remembered. Not only, "be a match," but his own words: "the earth is like a lover, who doesn't want to let you out of his bed."

He let his whole body go limp, and reached for Earth. And Earth received him. Earth held him.

"Fucking faggot! Stop resisting arrest!"

The cops tugged and pulled and swore, but Earth wouldn't let him go.

The power of Earth met the magic of the spiral, of the chanting, of the drums. Of breath, and rain, and every beating heart within the circle.

"Drop!" he shouted. His comrades grew heavy, Earth calling to flesh. They sank onto the ground, around him, arms still linked, heads held upward to the blessed kiss of rain. The two cops stumbled and slipped, scrambling to not fall on their asses at the sudden shifting weight.

He felt Aiden then. And Brigid. And the rapid spread of energy that tasted of magic. It snapped into the four corners and held, forming a barrier of protection over the whole camp and the linked people surrounding it.

And then the two cops let go of Tobias. Hands released their bruising grips. Helmets shifted away. They just. Let. Go.

Tobias inhaled in relief. It still hurt. He fought back a cough.

The line of riot cops took one step back. Then another. They just stood there. Tobias could see them through his swollen, slitted eyes. They stood their in their gas masks, and their padded gloves and vests, behind their shields.

Behind him, a powerful woman's voice split through the sound of rolling thunder, drums, and rain.

"Out here in the darkness, I'm gonna let it shine! Out here in the darkness, I'm gonna let it shine."

Lightning flickered.

The magic was working! *Aiden! It's working!* He hoped Aiden could feel this, wherever he was.

The heartbeat of the drum paused, then began again. There were voices in the center, chanting a counterpoint to the woman's song, in a language Tobias didn't recognize. It must be the Wasco Nation, chanting prayers.

Then more voices joined in from the circle and the camp. "Out here in the darkness, we're gonna let it shine!"

He felt a wash of love and safety surround him, covering them all. And then, the sweet scent of green grasses and fields of wheat.

"Brigid?" he whispered.

The singing went on and on. Tobias straightened up, and helped the people on either side of him sit up, too. The boundary circle righted itself.

"In the face of violence, we're gonna let it shine, let it shine, let it shine, let it shine!"

Tobias's face stung. His eyes and throat were filled with the sensation of sandpaper and glass.

"Tilt your head back," a voice behind him said.

"What?"

"Tilt your head back. I'm going to help you."

Tobias did, and flinched as the viscous liquid hit him. Antacid. Magnesium hydroxide and water. It washed the burn away.

"Open your eyes. I know it feels weird, but I'm going to pour some in."

Tobias opened his injured eyes as wide as he could, trying not to blink.

The singing went on and on around him.

The person behind him wiped his face.

"Better?" they asked.

The stinging receded.

"Better." He turned his head to see who'd been helping him. It was a small person wearing a gas mask. A red cross made of electrical tape graced the sleeves of their black jacket. May all the Gods bless anarchist field medics. "Thank you."

"No prob." The medic got up from their crouch and went to help the person next to him.

Tobias didn't know whether to laugh or cry. He felt wild, as though he could run through the rain, shrieking and dancing. But he also wanted to stay right here, linked to these beautiful people, for the rest of his life.

Tobias's skin and eyes still burned, but maybe, just maybe, he was going to be fine.

Maybe all of them were going to be fine.

The cops were leaving now, boots pounding on the street, heading away from Open Heart.

Unbelievable.

The camp set up a cheer.

38

AIDEN

The rain had stopped. The skies were still gray, but it was dry when he stepped outside. The air felt amazing on his skin. Aiden closed his eyes and inhaled.

Then he heard feet running up the steps.

"Aiden!" A familiar voice. He opened his eyes right before Tobias swept him into a bone crushing hug.

It hurt. But Aiden held on tight as they swayed back and forth, heads held close together, breathing in each other's scent. Frankincense. Myrrh. Fire. And something new. The scent of damp earth. Funny, that was what he would have expected an herbalist to smell like: earth and plants. He finally did.

Aiden looked over his lover's shoulder and saw a grinning troupe gathered at the bottom of the stairs. Stingray and Brad. Sister Jan. Barry and Sheila from the camp. Jaqueline and Rabbi Schwartz. Oh my God, even Reverend Laney was there to greet him.

"Yeah. Your fan club is here," Tobias said in his ear. "Want to say hello?"

Aiden kissed Tobias's neck. "I would."

As Tobias took his hand and walked Aiden down the steps to his friends, Aiden couldn't help but think of the men he'd left inside the jail. They were waiting to be transferred, waiting to be bailed out, waiting for a lawyer to advise them to cop a plea.

Waiting for the world to change.

But every last one of them had helped him. They had held up Brigid's mantle in that cramped and stinking cell. They had helped bring peace to the land. At least one small part of it.

He had blessed each man before he left. They clasped his hands, and gave him the nod that signified respect. They hadn't spoken much, because there was too much and too little to say. He'd told them to look him up at De Porres House if they ever needed him. For anything.

"Thanks, holy man, I will," one of them said. But Aiden couldn't tell if the man had meant it. Their fate was too uncertain, the only certainty being that they were likely getting the short end of the stick again. And again.

"Aiden! We're so glad they let you go!"

He started hugging everyone in turn. "Yeah, I was told the charges were dropped?"

"Yes," Sister Jan said. She had a purple hat on over her salt-and-pepper hair. The hat matched her Doc Martens eight-hole boots. Her blue eyes sparked behind big black-rimmed glasses.

"And what were the charges, exactly?" Aiden honestly didn't know. The whole time he'd been inside, he'd barely been present to his surroundings.

"Disturbing the peace and resisting arrest," Sister Jan replied.

"Resisting? I fainted. Or passed out. Or...I'm not exactly sure what happened."

Stingray shook her hands and tilted her head in an *I know, I know,* gesture. "They always want to charge people with that. He convinced them you were having a spiritual crisis."

Aiden looked toward where she was pointing, at an older, light skinned Black gentleman with a wispy mustache. He wore a long tan trench coat over a dark brown suit, matching leather briefcase in his left hand.

The man stepped forward.

"Hello, Aiden. My name is Walter Copley. I'm please to make your acquaintance."

"You got me out?"

"It's what I do."

Aiden wanted to shout down a raft of blessings on top of the man's thinning hair, but he didn't want to freak him out.

"Thank you," he said. "May I offer you a blessing?"

Walter looked startled, then gave a quick nod, and bowed his head.

Aiden placed his hands, palms down, so gently, resting over the lawyer's brow. He caught a whiff of pipe tobacco and paper.

"Brigid, as you have blessed me, and blessed this city, please bless this man. You offered me a choice of many things, and I chose the torch of illumination. I ask that you offer this man, Walter Copley, whatever illumination he chooses, and whatever blessing he needs."

He felt a warmth flowing through his palms, and onto Walter's head. Then it was done. He lifted up his hands, and Walter raised his head. There were tears shining in his eyes.

"How did you know?"

"I didn't. All I did was ask."

The man nodded, then reached into his coat pocket and pulled out a business card.

"If you ever need me again, I'll be around." Then he turned and walked away. Aiden watched him for a moment, looking at the slight halo of light around his head.

"We're taking you to lunch at Raquel's," Jaqueline said, her voice jerking Aiden back from wherever it was he'd been.

He still felt so in between, and wondered if life would always be this way, or if he'd go back to something close to normal once things died down.

Aiden looked at his friends and smiled.

"Raquel's sounds great. Tobias is always talking about how good those paninis are. And I want to hear all about what happened at the camp."

Reverend Laney cleared this throat. "I won't be able to go to lunch—there's a vestry meeting this afternoon. But I wanted to be here to greet you when you were released." He held out his right hand.

Aiden looked at it, then met it with his own. "Thanks for being here, Reverend."

"No. Thank you. Thank you for...everything."

"Come on, Aiden, I'm hungry," Stingray said. "And I didn't take the day off from the kitchen just to stand around on a cold sidewalk."

"Aiden?" Aiden turned. It was Terry Benson, from the city council. She approached rapidly, coat swinging out behind her. "I'm glad I caught you." She looked around the group. Everyone was silent. Waiting. "I want you to know that the city council is going to push to end the sweeps."

"How about the rest of it?" Tobias asked. "The mayor, the chief of police? Permanent encampments?"

She grimaced. "I'll deny ever saying this to you, but, one step at a time is my answer. One step at a time. And Aiden? Thank you. Thank all of you."

Then she hurried off.

"Well, that's a victory," Stingray said. "A small one, but I'll take what we can get. And right now, I hope that looks a lot like a ham and cheese panini."

Aiden threw an arm around Stingray's shoulders. "Lead on, crew chief. Lead on."

Turning his head, he saw Tobias smiling at him, goatee freshly trimmed, brown eyes so bright, though they were red around the edges, and a portion on his left cheek looked slightly burned. Aiden was sure there was a story there. He held out his other hand, and Tobias laced his fingers through his.

"Let's get you fed."

39

TOBIAS

Tobias blinked at his blue bedroom ceiling. He should probably turn on a light. Afternoon was rapidly turning into evening, and the gray light in the room was fading fast. Soft rain pattered outside. Tobias smelled the rosemary in the garden. And the herbs in the kitchen. And the trees.

The chemicals hadn't taken that away from him. His throat and eyes still felt a little raw, but whatever this new sense was that he had been gifted was still intact.

Goddess, the bed felt good, as did Aiden, curled around him. It felt as though the past week had taken a year.

Lunch had taken a year. They had sat in Raquel's cafe for hours. Too long.

There had been so much to catch up on. So many stories to tell. Tobias had a feeling they'd be unpacking everything that happened for months. Like, who had called off the cops, right when the magic snapped into place? Raquel told him to trust that sometimes, magic just worked, and how much more proof did he need?

And there were still the injunctions Walter Copley wanted to serve. The lawyer thought the protestors and the camp had a good case against the city, the mayor, and the police. Terry Benson's promises would help, Tobias hoped. But that was going to take years. The wheels of justice ground slowly.

Tobias wasn't sure if he was up for that sort of sustained, bureaucratic action, but he'd do whatever Aiden or the camp decided they wanted. The feeling of being surrounded by people, linked like that, stayed with him. He couldn't shake the solid sense of three hundred people having his back, and the knowledge that he had theirs.

He'd heard some activist-types call each other *comrade* before, and had thought it was a petty affectation. He didn't think that anymore.

The people who had held on to his body when the riot cops were trying to drag him away? They were his comrades now. His father would be horrified. That made Tobias feel just fine.

He was going to tell his father he was moving out of the house. He wasn't going to fight him anymore. Freddie and Reece could keep the place if they wanted it. His clients were right, he would raise his prices for those who could afford it. Or maybe set up a sliding scale. The money would come somehow.

Brigid had assured him he was a healer, and he figured that meant he could count on her help. The Gods and humans had a sacred pact, Brenda would say. That meant, if he served her as a healer, she'd take care of him, right?

Regardless of whether or not that was true, it was clear to him now that as a healer and a witch, he would keep step- ping up.

Besides, he had the visceral memory of Earth supporting him now. Earth wasn't going to let him go.

"What are you thinking?" Aiden's voice was sleepy.

"Shhh. Nothing. Go back to sleep."

Aiden settled himself, breathing growing deep and even again. Tobias felt him relax and grow heavy against his body, and smiled.

After the long lunch, and promises extracted that there would be a debrief with the coven, and the Interfaith Council, and, and, and, and, Tobias had dragged Aiden home. He had figured he'd just hold him while he slept. Goddess knew the man needed some rest. Tobias, too.

Aiden had surprised him that afternoon. As soon as Tobias shut his bedroom door, Aiden was on him, tugging up his sweater, and unbuckling his belt.

"What happened to your raincoat, anyway?" Aiden asked in the middle of the frantic undressing. "You look like you have new clothes."

"Yeah," Tobias replied, pulling a long sleeved T-shirt over Aiden's head. "My clothes got wrecked by the teargas. Stuff that couldn't be washed five times got sealed into a garbage bag and thrown away. I couldn't even wear anything into the house. My housemates made me change out on the porch."

"In front of the neighbors?" Aiden practically shrieked, stopping in the middle of pulling off his jeans.

"In front of the neighbors. They wouldn't even give me a towel, just made me run through the house naked to the shower."

"Wow."

Then they were kissing. Then they were climbing onto the high bed, practically dragging each other onto the mattress. Then they were climbing all over each other, and under each other. Then Aiden was staring at him with those big blue eyes.

Tobias started crying. They didn't stop making love even then, though it grew tender for a time, then fierce again.

It was the sweetest, hottest sex Tobias had ever experienced in his life.

Tobias sighed, content. The only thing he needed right now was a drink to ease his throat.

Gently sliding his way out from underneath his lover, Tobias got up to get some water from the bathroom.

When he came back into the shadowy bedroom, the slice of light from the hallway showed Aiden, awake and sitting up in bed. He was staring at the altar, a look of rapture on his face. Tobias closed the door quietly, and set the water glass down on the bedside table. Then he walked naked to the altar, drew out a tiny box of matches, and struck the red head of one on the slice of sandpaper on the lid. The match head flared, and sulfur hit his nose.

He touched the flame to the wick of a beeswax taper, and shook out the flaming match.

"Holy Brigid, we honor you. We give you thanks."

He heard the creak of the bed, then felt a soft touch as Aiden came to stand behind him, pressing his chest and hip to Tobias's shoulder and ass. He felt his breath, and smelled that special Aiden scent of him.

Tobias took another breath. "Holy Brigid, we ask of you..." What did he want to say?

"To bless our relationship," Aiden said, wrapping his arms around Tobias's waist.

Yes.

"To bless our path. And to help us continue to forge justice from the fires of love." Tobias completed the prayer and turned in his lover's arms, until they faced each other once again.

Then he lowered his face to Aiden's, and sucked his lower lip between his own.

Aiden gave a slight moan, and kissed him back. Then he led Tobias back to bed.

REVIEWS

Reviews can make or break a book's success.
If you enjoyed this book, please consider telling a friend, or
leaving a short review at your favorite booksellers or on
GoodReads.
Many thanks!

READ AN EXCERPT OF BY WIND

BY WIND, CHAPTER ONE

The first pangs of a headache started at the base of Brenda's skull. It felt like pressure, building up inside of her, waiting to burst free. Or crush her in its wake.

Don't be so dramatic, she thought. *It's just a change in barometric pressure or something.*

Except the sky was blue today. There wasn't any storm on the horizon.

As a matter of fact, Brenda *should* feel energized. This was her time of year. It was almost Vernal Equinox, and the moon was waxing toward half. Everything should feel as if it was tipping toward balance, but instead, everything felt wrong.

She needed balance this year, more than ever. Portland did, too, after the scandals that had rocked local government during the fall and winter. Scandals that Arrow and Crescent Coven had been smack in the middle of.

The sun was out, though the cold rains would be back soon, Brenda was sure. But today was one of those perfect April days when people pretended it was warm enough to leave their heavy coats at home and venture out only in a sweater or light jacket.

She should have felt awesome. Instead, it took everything she had to pay attention to the customers, and to keep her psychic shields up and at the ready. The headache made both almost impossible.

The Inner Eye was busy for a Wednesday, late morning. Not jammed, but there were several people browsing the books, gems, divination tools, and herbs.

Lead crystals in the windows caught the sunlight and refracted it into tiny rainbows that danced throughout the store. Brenda tried to soothe her jangled nerves and increasing pain by humming along to Loreena McKennitt's voice and harp.

Tempest, her part-time worker and full-time coven sister, walked toward the back room, with a box of books UPS had just delivered. They would need pricing. This month, the back and sides of Tempest's head were shaved, and a straight fall of teal hair fell down around her delicate face.

"Can't we listen to something other than this caterwauling?"

Tempest was a gifted massage therapist and also a young smart-ass.

"No. The customers like it." Brenda had loved this album since it was new. She didn't care how many years ago that was. It made her feel like her best, most witchy self, even on days like today, when she really wanted to crawl back into bed with an old favorite book, like one of Charles de Lint's.

It was weird that she felt in such need of comfort. She wondered what was coming. What was wrong.

The bells over the door rang, and young Black man, dressed neatly in a red windbreaker, a retro Run-DMC T-shirt and skinny jeans over Chuck Taylor sneakers looked around, and approached the counter.

"Um...do you have any Palo Santo?" he asked.

Brenda smiled. "I do. Just got some in, as a matter of fact."

She scanned the shelves on the wall, behind the counter, eyes searching the large glass jars. "I put it on this shelf just yesterday..." she muttered. "Tempest? Did you move the Palo Santo?"

Tempest came back, sans box of books. "Yes! Sorry! I took it down for another customer this morning, got busy, and forgot to put it back. It's here."

The jar was down at the end of the long glass display counter, tucked behind some other jars that also needed re-shelving. She held it out to Brenda.

:*The wood reveals the seeker's heart. The young man needs not only cleansing, but protection. Care for him well, before the light around him dims.*:

Brenda almost dropped the jar. That was *not* her intuition, her inner psychic voice. That wasn't even one of her usual spirit guides. It was an actual, practically physically audible, voice inside her head. What the...?

"Whoa!" Tempest said, catching hold of the jar again. "I didn't realize you didn't have it yet before I let go. Sorry about that!"

Brenda shook her head. "It's fine. My fault."

Tempest gave her a look, but didn't say a word, just turned to show some Tarot decks to a couple of Goth teens, their already white skin made paler by black lipstick and layers of black eye makeup.

Brenda took a breath, trying to quiet the sudden inner turmoil, and turned to the young man. "Do you know what size stick you need? I can pour some out for you, so you can choose."

He looked slightly uncomfortable. "Um...I'm not sure. I've never bought any before. Someone just told me it was good...."

His voice trailed off, as if he was embarrassed to be talking about it.

Brenda opened the jar and shook out several pieces of the fragrant wood, inhaling the scent. It was one of her favorites. Palo Santo wood was slightly sweet, smelling of frankincense and copal.

"It's good for cleansing," she said, briskly. She found that if customers were ill at ease, it was best to act as though every single thing in the shop was ordinary, as though it could be found anywhere. She dropped her voice then, fingers playing over the pale, jagged sticks, careful to not look at the young man's face. "Some people also use it for various types of healing work. They say it's good for easing certain types of depression and anxiety."

She looked up again, brightening her expression. "So, do any of these sticks appeal?"

He turned each one over, carefully, fingers sliding across the wood. "I don't know. Does it matter?"

He finally looked up at her, and she could see the fear and confusion in his eyes.

"It only matters to you," she said, putting a slight push of power behind her words. "Everything you choose should be because you want it."

He breathed in sharply. Then shook his head. "If only."

"Don't let them do that to you."

"What?" He backed away from the counter.

Damn. She shouldn't have said that. *Don't scare the customers*, Brenda. She could feel Tempest staring at her, likely wondering what the heck was up. Non-consensual psychic reading. Rookie mistake.

She held her hands up, palms out, in a placating gesture.

"I'm sorry. I wasn't fishing around in your brain, I promise. It's just that sometimes I get hits. Psychic information." She'd already messed up by saying something, so might as well say some more. "And it feels like someone is trying to make you feel like nothing you do will help. I don't know who those people are, but I don't think that's true. I think you have a lot to offer. It's all around you. In your aura."

He kept backing up, slowing, almost crashing into a display of crystals and gemstones. Luckily, he caught himself and veered into the aisle.

"I'm sorry," Brenda said. "I didn't mean to scare you."

She held up a stick of Palo Santo, the first one her hand touched. "Let me give this to you. Please."

He shook his head. "No. Thanks." Then turned and left the store. The bells jingled him out the door. Brenda sighed, scooped the blond shards of wood back into the glass jar, and snapped the lid closed.

Then she put it in its place back on the shelf where it belonged. Something buzzed at the back of her brain. That phrase, "Where it belonged." There was something about the young man...as though he was out of place. No. As if part of his soul was out of place.

Well, that happened sometimes. People gave parts of themselves away to others all the time, actually. It was why soul retrieval was necessary. She just didn't like doing it. It made her sad to have to seek out lost shards of soul like that. Even though reunion should have been a happy thing, something was always different when the piece of a soul came home again.

"It's just change, Brenda. Everything goes through it," she said.

"What's that?" Tempest said from right behind her.

Brenda jumped a little. What was *wrong* with her today?

"Sorry. Just talking to myself. Did those girls buy anything?"

Tempest gave her another look. "Yeah. They wanted to look at the Thoth deck, but frankly, they're not ready for the study it requires yet."

"Sometimes that's how we learn, Tempest. You know that."

"Yeah, yeah. I sold them one anyway. But they also wanted Brian Froud's Faerie Oracle. I figured that even though it's not really Tarot, it'll help teach them how to use the cards in general."

Brenda smiled. The Faerie Oracle was a strange deck, and seemed lighthearted at first, but wasn't really, not when you got right down to it. Brian and Wendy Froud were amazing artists, and Brenda knew they had some real magic between them.

"They also took a flier for the pendulum class. Did you miss this?" Tempest asked, holding up a piece of Palo Santo.

"Damn. I guess I did."

Tempest reached for the jar. Brenda stopped her. "No. Clearly we need to burn it in the shop today. Our usual incense isn't clearing the space well enough. The spirits seem to want something different today."

She just hoped that wasn't an omen. She really just wanted to enjoy this spring.

But for now, there was work to do. She bustled over to a white woman wearing blue jeans and a long, burgundy sweater, who had been steadily taking book after book off the shelf, and was now plopped into one of the two damask reading chairs, looking thoroughly confused.

"Were you looking for something in particular?" she asked.

The woman looked up at her, brown eyes stricken, furrows running alongside her mouth and a crease between her eyebrows.

"I need help," she said. "But I just don't know what kind."

And then she burst into tears.

ACKNOWLEDGMENTS

I give thanks to the cafés of my new hometown, Portland, Oregon. All you baristas are fine human beings.

Thanks also to Leslie Claire Walker, my intrepid first reader, to Dayle Dermatis, editor extraordinaire, to Lou Harper for my covers, and to my writing buddies for getting me out of the house.

Speaking of house...thanks as always to Robert and Jonathan.

Big, grateful shout out to the members of the Sorcery Collective for spreading the word!

And last...

Thanks to all the activists and witches working your magic in the world. This series is for you.

ABOUT THE AUTHOR

T. Thorn Coyle has been arrested at least four times. Buy her a cup of tea or a good whisky and she'll tell you about it.

Author of the *The Witches of Portland*, the alt-history urban fantasy series *The Panther Chronicles*, the novel *Like Water*, and two story collections, her multiple non-fiction books include *Sigil Magic for Writers, Artists & Other Creatives*, and *Evolutionary Witchcraft*.

Thorn's work appears in many anthologies, magazines, and collections. She has taught magical practice in nine countries, on four continents, and in twenty-five states.

An interloper to the Pacific Northwest U.S., Thorn stalks city streets, writes in cafes, loves live music, and talks to crows, squirrels, and trees.

Connect with Thorn:
www.thorncoyle.com

ALSO BY T. THORN COYLE

Fiction Series

The Panther Chronicles

To Raise a Clenched Fist to the Sky

To Wrest Our Bodies From the Fire

To Drown This Fury in the Sea

To Stand With Power on This Ground

The Witches of Portland

By Earth

By Flame

By Wind

By Sea

Single Novels and Story Collections

Like Water

Alighting on His Shoulders

Break Apart the Stone

Anthologies

Fantasy in the City

Haunted

Witches Brew

The Faerie Summer

Stars in the Darkness

Fiction River: Justice

Fiction River: Feel the Fear

Non-Fiction

Evolutionary Witchcraft

Kissing the Limitless

Make Magic of Your Life

Sigil Magic for Writers, Artists & Other Creatives

Crafting a Daily Practice

Made in the USA
San Bernardino, CA
20 November 2018